Tunnel Runner

A Novel by:

Richard Sand

To Loni –
go NAIBA!

Library of Congress Cataloging-in-Publication Data Sand, Richard, 1943-

Tunnel Runner / by Richard Sand

Library of Congress Catalog Card Number: 00-105975

p. cm.

ISBN 1-930754-02-7

First Edition

10 9 8 7 6 5 4 3 2 1

Visit our Web site at http://www.durbanhouse.com

Thank you to John and Karen Lewis,
and Sgt. Raymond Wright, USMC, Deceased. And
for my children, Peter, Miriam, Jake, and Luke,
and my wife, Kathie, who I have loved forever.

Tunnel Runner

A Novel by:

Richard Sand

The Elms

The hunter, the hero, the killer, lay paralyzed in a strange bed. Ashman woke and fell asleep over and over in the square white room. There was no sense of time for him. There was just the rushing warmth of the drugs that carried him away. Ashman began to separate from himself in floating parts.

At first, there were just parts of things that made no sense. At last, he dreamt that he was in combat again, running over the battleground or under it, running to save his life or take another's with his jungle knife or hidden gun. Then Ashman heard noises in his room and down the hall. He heard bits of conversations and doggerel singing ,but drifted away without finishing his thoughts or learning where he was.

Ashman needed answers to get out. Soon, he knew he was getting oxygen and an I.V. But he couldn't speak or move. He tried to separate his dream world from the real world, but they became each other again and again. The drugs took Ashman out on their waves and he went spinning away.

It was cruelest for Ashman when he awoke from dreaming that he was fighting or escaping or that he had come to the end of a tunnel to a flowering avenue, and then realized that he could not move. Even when he figured a subtle way out and willed it into his dreams, it did not work. He asked himself, Am I badly hurt? Who put me here, brought me here? Is it a betrayal taking me down, or vengeance from an unknown enemy? He had no answers and could not move.

They came and changed his I.V. bag again. Like all the other times, Ashman could not see them. He thought he heard things, but it told him nothing. The warm drug waves rolled into his mouth and he thought they would drown him. He tried to fight by squeezing his eyes so hard that his brain flashed with exploding lights, but he could not stop the sleep that choked him. Ashman thought he was drowning in a flooding Vietnam tunnel that he was in thirty years ago. Then he fell into a memory of sharp, high grass and ladders going up that he could not reach.

Ashman woke with a metal taste in his mouth. It was bitter and he could not spit it out. Headaches came which cut and tore his brain. This time when they came to give him the drugs, he was glad for it. Ashman hated himself for that, knowing if he embraced the comfort, he would be lost forever.

The crashing, tearing, headaches came three more times. Ashman prayed to be carried away. The headaches stopped and the warmth stopped. New dreams came, more awful, more cruel, more cunning. They drenched him with all the terror and the horror he had ever known. Bags with the severed heads of once good friends, feeding rats, betrayal in the night. Ashman screamed, but no sound came out.

Then there was horror in his dreaming like the terror in his waking. Ashman dreamt that he ran along a long hall with no doors. The hall got narrower and narrower as he ran, so that he could not move. The walls and the ceilings became each other and pressed down on him so that he could not breathe. There was no escape.

* * *

There were tunnels under the building at the Elms Residential Hospital. They were to keep the patients dry when they were moved from building to building, and to hide them from the public view. Nash, who lived and worked there, thought it was so the patients wouldn't drown from looking up like turkeys in the rain. Nash got off his box of lettuce in the tunnel and took it back up to the kitchen.

Big O'Dell was sitting outside the kitchen on a white wicker chair, smoking his after lunch cigar. He was blowing the smoke straight up so his graying beard and clothes didn't smell from it. "I thought you forgot about the box," Big O'Dell told Nash, "I need the lettuce to make salads green."

Nash put the box down and went to eat his lunch. He thought the heads of lettuce smiled at him.

He went outside and got his lunch which Big O'Dell had left for him on an outside shelf with the last slice of pie in an aluminum plate. Nash ate it all on the cardboard sheet he set upon the ground so that all that World was his, and all the while he sang a secret song.

When Big O'Dell rang the bell, Nash knew it was time to go back to work. He took off his plastic eating gloves and put on his plastic cleaning gloves and put away his cardboard and took his new aluminum plate to place in his room with the others. Nash got his cleaning cart and changed his song from the eating one to the cleaning one, which got louder as he went along.

He followed the hallway on the second floor, staying to the outside. There were three single rooms together in a line, and one was around another corner. Nash went down the row fast, but not running, until he came to the corner which he turned slowly.

Even though the first room was empty, Nash shot the blue germ killer in the bowl and sink. He wiped all the corners, the square ones first, and then the round ones, from the outside in, towards the center of the room where he stood in his yellow boots when he was done.

Nash went in and cleaned Ashman's room as he did each day. But this time when he was done with the cleaning and his singing, he came close to the bed. Ashman was defenseless. He waited, watching and vulnerable. The cleaning man, who smelled liked cooked onions, turned the bed a bit and mopped under it. The disinfectant smell was strong. With the bed turned, Ashman could see around the window shade to the world outside.

The next day Ashman could hear Nash's cleaning cart go down the hall. By the way the cart sound traveled, he could tell that the hall turned somewhere after his room. Later, he heard a fire bell.

The following morning, Ashman could move his tongue. It

was the first thing he could move since he found himself in the strange bed. Ashman could not speak, but he licked his upper lip. There was a moustache there now.

When the night came, he felt that "hostiles" were in the trees above and behind him so that he ran in his dream to run the razor wire all around his room. Inside the wire was Laura Beth, who he had not seen for thirty years. "I raised your bed," she said, sounding like President Johnson's wife and smiling widely, but with her teeth moving back and forth. "Shall I fluff your pillow? Fluff, fluff. Yes, doesn't my face look a bit more fluffed? I'm afraid I may have the wrong room. But I will see you again soon," she said. "Do you tango? Do you copy? Do you copy, Tango Alpha Bravo?"

Ashman fell asleep. He woke and slept in broken parts. When he awoke again, the cleaning man was there. Nash stopped his doggerel singing as he was about to wheel his cleaning cart outside. He turned to face the bed, "You should have killed them all," he said.

Escape

Nash thought the night noises at the Elms Residential Hospital were mountain goats running along the edges of the mountains in the dark, and owls calling, and mountain lions crying. He ate a small pie outside before he went into his room and locked himself in. Nash was proud to lock his door with the key he kept around his neck on a string.

In the morning while the others slept, he unlocked his room and went into the cool tunnel and went down and around, following the narrow path between the lines of high back chairs that used to crowd the upstairs hallways. Some of the chairs still had their original leather straps and black metal wheels attached.

Nash went there twice a day to see the people who had left the hospital and come back and those who had never left. He sat on his yellow and white chair and told a story to the ones in the tunnel as they sat on their mattresses or ran around with their arms flapping. When Nash told the story, he believed a hawk was over his head and in the back towards the right. He felt it at his ear as he told the story about a silver man and mountain goats with talking horns. And when the story was done, he went up to work, looking backwards as he did.

"Clack, clack," said one of those remaining in the tunnel, "clack, clack." He walked on, making the shape of secret eights in his steps and in endless circles in his hair. The others left behind rocked back and forth or ran into the dark.

Nash walked around above the tunnel. Ashman saw his red coat and yellow boots in the angled space that bordered the window shade in his square white room.

Ashman counted his days by the light outside that shade and by the fact that Nash came once a day to clean his room. Six days had passed since he was first able to see past the window shade. It rained one of the days and he saw Nash's red coat twice. On the rainy day, Ashman smelled wet wool and aftershave. Then deep sleep took him away.

When he awoke, he could smell the aftershave again. Old Spice, Ashman thought. And he thought he smelled a cigar, not a cheap one, perhaps a Macanudo, on the part of his pillow closest to the door. Either the doctor rested his hand on the pillow or the night nurse who attended to his I.V. bag, smoked cigars.

Ashman thought of ways to make that distinction as he turned his eyes towards the space near the shade to see outside. The shade was pulled straight and closed. He could not see. They had taken away the world outside.

Ashman felt anger and as it grew, his terror left. It buoyed him and he thought about escape and revenge.

He knew that the shade had been closed for three days because the cleaning man had come three more times. Ashman also knew that the doctor or the night nurse was male because he had smelled no lotion or perfume and he had smelled the cigar smell again.

Nash came in singing. The song made no sense. He cleaned the bathroom, squirting the blue killer in the bowl and wiping the whole room down toward the center point of his yellow boots.

Then Nash told Ashman a story. It was about stars and shining fish. The stars were falling down and turning on their arms. The fish were falling and going up and down and going splash. Nash said, "splash" over and over. He seemed to get agitated and when he left, he was still saying it.

Nash came back, the second time that day, and closed the door. With Ashman motionless and paralyzed, he pulled back the blankets and took Ashman's penis in his hand.

Shock and pain seared Ashman as the sweating, cleaning man yanked out the catheter. "Whee!" yelled Nash, as he ran to the head of the bed and back again. He grabbed Ashman and pulled him onto the cleaning cart. "Splash!" he yelled.

They were out of the room and down the hall fast, the cleaning cart careening around the corner with Ashman feeling heavy and weak and free. The I.V. bag was dragging and his blood was running down into it. He could see the ceiling had recessed fluorescent lights and then part of the walls and doors. Then they stopped.

Nash grabbed the canvas strap and pulled the elevator door open. He pushed the cleaning cart in. The I.V. bag caught in the door. Nash pulled it free and threw it up onto Ashman. The bleeding slowed.

Ashman was wheeled through a big iron door and into the tunnels, left, left, right, left. He lost consciousness again. When he awoke, he was sitting on a beach chair. He pulled the I.V. out and pressed the wound.

There was a pitcher of iced tea near his right hand. It was a red and white pitcher. Ashman could smell the sweet contents. There was a double bulb overhead. A long electrical cord ran down the tunnel wall. Ashman was cold and wearing fuzzy blue slippers.

He tried to get out of the chair, but his balance could not hold him. He swooned and fell back, but after a rest he was able to stand. His arms and legs hurt. His hands were slow.

Ashman knew that he had to move quickly, that his time was running out. He went towards the left, ambling and shuffling as he tried to run, wondering whether he might have lost count of the twists and turns Nash had taken. But he had been in tunnels before and ran on.

His limbs felt heavy and the blood running into his hands and feet made them hurt, but his strength was coming back. There was an iron ladder ahead and he made for it.

Out of the corner of his eye, Ashman saw the movement of flapping arms and a dirty, bald-headed man coming fast toward the ladder. Ashman angled at him from behind, and took him down at his knees. The man's face was filled with craziness and hate. Ashman jabbed him in the eye and smashed him in the temple with his elbow. The man stayed down and rolled away, gagging and crying.

Ashman took his yellow pants. Inside were $5.16, some stones, and a piece of gum. When the bald man started to sit up, he kicked him in the head and took his shoes, and shirt. The shirt pocket held a string, a piece of chicken, and a nail. Ashman thought of finishing him, but let him be.

Ten minutes later, Ashman was heading north in a blue Jeep Cherokee he had hot-wired from the hospital parking lot. There was a half a tank of gas and some change in the console. He knew he needed at least another fifty dollars to get far enough away to get a good read on things and get his strength back.

Ashman ditched the jeep and took a Buick at a rest stop on the turnpike. He drove on to the next stop, went in and out, and pulled to the shoulder of the road. When no one came, Ashman backed up and went in to get gas, take a piss, and feed himself.

It burned and bled from the catheter and he had to grab the urinal to hold on. Ashman could see someone staring at him in the mirror. The man was about fifty and had a puffy face and good clothes. He was trolling for sex.

Ashman went into a stall and waited, holding the door open a bit with his foot. The man came in.

"Fifty bucks," Ashman told him.

"Oh, yes," the man said as he went to his knees.

"Money first."

"Oh, yes."

Ashman reached out and took the yearning man's head in his hands. He kneed him in the face, breaking his nose, then choked him out.

Blood had splattered on his pants and down onto one of his shoes. He took the man's trousers along with his wallet, watch, and car keys. After cleaning up, he drove away to rest and set-up.

Ashman had been out of the World for the time he was at the Elms. He needed an explanation for that piece of his life that he had lost. Whoever put him in the mental hospital would pay for it. To Ashman, revenge was not an indulgence, but a necessity.

Eggs Doyle

Ashman's anger swelled, but he knew to watch his speed as he put distance and confusion between him and those who would be coming after him. Although the route he had chosen was direct, he left the highway often.

After three more hours of driving, he pulled into an adult entertainment center, hot wired the most expensive car in the parking lot, and left his Buick in its spot. By the time the owner came out and discovered his Cadillac was not there and then decided he should call the police, Ashman had gone back to the interstate and was miles away.

Acting on his plan for escape and revenge kept Ashman sharp, but he knew that he was physically weak and that his adrenaline high would not last. He hoped it would get him to Buffalo, where he could set up a base camp at Doyle's.

"Eggs" Doyle had been his friend for twenty-five years.

They had first met in Thailand. Ashman was the resident contact man there, having left his military service for the CIA. "Same job, better pay, better clothes, and you get to shit indoors," his CIA recruiter had told him. Doyle had been sent by a private security company, to bring back a Dupont executive strung-out on opium and thirteen year old prostitutes.

They met again ten years later in D.C. Doyle was still working for National Executive Services. He brought Ashman into NES, where they worked together for six years before Ashman went back to government work.

"Eggs" was always good for him. They had been through life and death together, the mud and blood, they called it, but even so, Ashman wanted to watch Doyle first. He surveilled Doyle's house and business and then followed him out over the narrow causeway.

His old friend shook him loose, but Ashman knew where he was going and picked him up there, finding Doyle's red Cadillac parked half into the woods. Ashman could see a burly, bald man sitting on the ground. He was eating pickled eggs from a glass jar, his back against the white inside of the car door. Two stray dogs ran by him and around the empty picnic tables to pull at the green wire trash cans.

Doyle ate five eggs and then carried the egg jar into the woods. He emerged a few minutes later with the jar filled with water and drove away. Ashman followed him back over the causeway, keeping two and sometimes three cars between them. When the big finned Cadillac turned to go around the corner to the back of 'Kelly's Sure Thing,' Doyle's neighborhood bar, Ashman made a U-turn and drove passed the front. It looked like the neon sign still had not been repaired.

Ashman thought about Franca. They had been lovers and she was only twenty minutes away. Doyle's bar wasn't open yet. Ashman wanted to see her, but he knew he needed recon before that too.

He drove to her house in his reconnaissance and his memory. The route came alive. He passed the diner, the old Esso station with the red Pegasus sign, the quarries, and then the front of Franca's development.

All the houses looked alike with their faux facades and picture windows. He stopped outside Franca's house, which had been their home. It was still the last one next to an open field. He thought he could hear the tall clock chiming in the small parlor off the hall. Part of him wanted to sit with Franca on the green glider on the back porch. They used to sit and watch the night come onto the open land behind her house, the sky turning purple, before the black.

Franca came out to get her newspaper. That was not enough for Ashman and it was too much. She hadn't changed and Ashman wished he hadn't come. He drove away and went to get something to eat. The restaurant was gone, replaced by a dental supply house.

Ashman was exhausted. His hands and arm hurt and he knew he had to sleep because his judgment was weakening. He saw a motel ahead and checked in. The shower was a good one, and the hot pulsating water helped him relax. He wanted a cold beer, but settled for a Dr. Pepper and cheese balls from the vending machines in the hall. It was dark when Ashman awoke and went to see Doyle.

"I'm just closin'," the door man with the huge ring of keys told Ashman. His name was Jim Finnegan and he was big and beefy. Although the doorman wore his watch on his right hand, his muscle structure told Ashman that he was probably right handed. His red hair and pale skin said that he'd cut easy.

"I want to see Doyle."

"Closed," the big doorman said as he turned his back.

"Tell Doyle that Mutzy's here."

"I ain't no singing telegram. Youse'll have to come back."

Ashman could see the muscles in the man's right shoulder tense. "Wait," he said.

"Fuck you," Finnegan answered.

"Doyle's snake goin' get you."

Finnegan started to turn around, then thought better about it, and went for his boss. "Wait here."

Ashman gave the doorman his respect and waited. He could smell the beer and bar smell as the door opened. The jukebox was playing Tony Bennett, but there was no conversation.

Finnegan came back. "C'mon," he said.

Ashman went in. He could see the bald head of his friend, who was kneeling behind the bar. The place was the same except some of the tables and the chairs were new. There was a big screen TV, but it wasn't turned on.

"Hey, Mutz," said Doyle as he stood up.

Doyle looked like he always had, except his face was more puffy and he moved with less agility when he walked over.

Doyle started to put his arms around Ashman, but stopped. "Hey, Mutz," Doyle repeated. "Sit down, sit down."

They walked over to the corner table near the jukebox. Doyle was wearing his thick cowboy belt with the bronco on the buckle. Ashman knew the buckle contained a derringer .22.

"You wanta beer? I always have a beer at night. Helps me piss," Doyle told him. He went to the bar and drew two drafts and punched in a Shirley Bassey song.

They talked about the good old days, and gave each other updates. The Goldberg twins were dead. Warnock was married to two different women and living in Costa Rica. Bernsie had beaten prostate cancer and owned a hardware store in Baltimore.

"I saw Doc about eighteen months ago," Doyle went on. "He was in ICU in Bethesda. Threw a clot. He's doing ops at age sixty-two. God bless him. Anyways, suddenly I hear a scream and his wife, you know her, she comes running out of the room. 'He's not there! He's not there!' she's yelling. We all go in, the nurse, some dot head doc, me and her. There's Doc on the floor on the other side of the bed, doing friggin' push-ups and his gown is half off and he is going up and down, up and down, his round ass salutin' us."

They laughed and when they could think of no one else to talk about, they were quiet for a while.

"Dessert, like the old times," Doyle announced. He went into the kitchen. It was 2 a.m., like the old times.

Ashman got another beer. Finnegan was sweeping up, but stopped when Ashman went behind the bar. He started again when he saw what Ashman was doing.

Doyle cracked a half-dozen eggs into a bowl of Irish whiskey. He whipped the mixture and poured it into a black iron skillet, cooking it fast. He drizzled maple syrup on the eggs, and brought them out with a stack of white bread. "No sausages, Mutz," he said.

They settled on some ham. The two men ate without talking. Ashman belched after the second beer and acknowledged the name of the feast when they were done, "'Eggs Doyle'. God damn."

Doyle wiped up his syrup with the last piece of bread. "Fox or hound?" he asked.

"Little of both. Do I look that bad?"

"You look like shit. I got a room upstairs. Nobody bothers me anymore. I think everybody forgot about me, which is fine with me." He rubbed his head. "I used to think I was being watched all the time. Then I figured I was nuts, but it didn't matter either way. I kind of have that feeling in the background all the time, like radio static or somethin'. A while ago, The Eyes were all around the neighborhood, including a blonde chick. Can you believe that, ladies doing FBI fieldwork? No wonder they fucked up at Waco and Ruby Ridge. They didn't come in here though. Funny thing, when they're here, that background noise stops.

Anyways, the missus goes to bed early. She's still got the ears of a wolf on the prowl. We bought the place next door so she wouldn't have to put up with the bar noise. She's in the back. Had a breast removed a couple of years ago." He shook his head. "Still my girl, though. Saved my bacon. I'd be long dead or something."

Doyle looked away for a moment. "Our boy died a couple of years ago. Killed in his truck by a drunk driver. The bastard never made it to trial. I'll kill him again when I see him in Hell. Anyways, the Bureau, the Company, all of them, you know, they're a bunch of kiss-ass, fat ass, no guts, no honor sissies, all of 'em. Even NES got so corporate and chicken-shit that you'd puke. Us spies and bushwackers had to report to a damned Human Relations Officer. Wouldn't trust any of them to take out the trash, none of them alphabet soups, FBI, CIA, NES, what not. They're all pricks and pussies at the same time."

He called Finnegan over, telling him, "Meet my partner."

The big man came over and shook Ashman's hand. Then he went to get them coffee and to take out the trash.

They were finishing their coffee when Doyle told Ashman he had spoken to Franca. He had seen her at the mall and then she had called him two weeks ago, just small talk. Doyle went behind the bar to do the dishes, while Ashman sat on a stool in front.

"Packin'?" Doyle asked him.

"In between," Ashman answered.

Doyle reached beside the register and pulled out a Beretta .380. "Clean piece, and good, Mutz, the 85F. But can you believe the United States Army carries sidearms made by the Italians? Somewhere Mussolini is laughing," he said as he handed over the automatic.

When they went upstairs he tossed Ashman a pocket-sized,

double-action .32 caliber which he was carrying in his shirt. "Mutz, get some sleep. I'm goin next door. Can't sleep without her. Big Jim, my nephew, the guy who let you in, sleeps in the front room. He's good people. Anyways, stay as long as you want. The alarm code is 3274. Can you believe we got an alarm? There's towels in the hall."

Doyle threw his work shirt and apron in the bin as he went back down the corridor. Ashman could see the old tattoos on his back. They were faded, but he knew them, the dragon and the eagle and the snake coiling around and going down his old friend's back.

"Yeah, Mutz, them animals, I still got 'em," Doyle said. He kept walking. "Anyways, it beats having them on the inside."

Ashman walked around the second floor so he knew where the windows and doors were. After he washed up, he placed his guns where he could reach them and went to sleep on the floor on the far side of the bed which he had turned at a right angle.

He slept longer than he had wanted to. When Ashman awoke, he went downstairs. There was a note from Doyle saying him and Jim Finnegan had gone for bar supplies and that he could use his wife's green caddy. This meant that Doyle had gotten rid of the car that Ashman had stolen for his ride in.

He took the green Cadillac and drove the tourists' route past Niagara Falls, the Maid of the Mist, and over to the Horseshoe Falls. Ashman walked around the area twice before sitting down in front of the big floral clock.

Ashman thought about how he'd go back and straighten things out, but he knew he needed information first. He decided to see if Doyle could help him get some blood work, which might provide answers as to what and who had put him in the hospital.

Taking the old way back to the bar, Ashman stopped at Leone's to get sausages for Doyle. Mrs. Leone gave him a warm hello, but she must have been eighty and even though she nodded and smiled when he came in and left, Ashman doubted she recognized him or could remember.

When he got back to Doyle's, he parked the green Cadillac next door and walked over to the bar. Doyle's car was there, but the place was locked. Ashman knew something was wrong. He went around back. A window was broken. He went in combat-ready, toe, sole, heel, with the Beretta in his hands.

Jim Finnegan was lying face up behind the bar. He had been shot twice. Doyle was dead in the hall. A shotgun blast had torn away his shirt. There were pellet wounds everywhere. Ashman thought for a moment that it was the animals on Doyle's back that were bleeding. Bloody tears ran from them.

He took Doyle's .45 which was still in his belt, slid the safety off, and went room to room. The touch pad of the alarm had been ripped out of the wall and put in a bucket of water. The front door had been pried open. The register was open. It looked like a second-rate burglary, but it didn't feel that way.

Ashman went through the place again. Finnegan's room showed that he was ex-Navy. Doyle had family pictures in his office and a holster under his desk for the .45. Upstairs there was a passageway connecting the bar to the building next door where Doyle lived. The house was locked and secure. Ashman checked the bar's basement. It was clear.

He thought about Doyle's wife, but there was nothing he could do there. Ashman left in Finnegan's car and went directly to Franca's. She was the only connection to anything local. Doyle had mentioned her and he had just driven by her house. Something wasn't right.

Indian Country

The open field behind Franca's house ran two hundred yards to a macadam road. There were tall trees at the roadside and an unpaved road up from the macadam. Ashman and Franca had sat on the glider on the back porch, watching the trees in the wind and the night coming down. There was thistle and clover which brought bees during the day. In the evening there were fireflies, night birds, and bats that swooped down and around.

Now Ashman saw the open field as a killing ground. He quickly crossed the space up to the back porch, the .45 in his right hand and the Beretta in his belt for back-up. He had stashed the .32 pocket piece under the dashboard of his car, which he had parked on the close side of the trees. Ashman wasn't sure why he was there, but what he was doing felt right.

He noted that the holly bushes had grown high in the back. They would be noisy and sharp. The glider was gone. He wondered what kind of alarm system was installed. The screen door was partially open. He couldn't see the dog and would have to be careful of it coming up behind him. Then Ashman realized that he had been gone so long that Franca's dog was probably dead. He wondered if she had gotten another one.

Silently, Ashman went into the breakfast room. He could smell coffee and maybe cigarette smoke. Not hers. She hated it. The kitchen clock was the same. He could see into the den, which still had the purple wallpaper arching up towards the ceiling. The couch was different.

He heard a radio playing and from the corner of his right eye, towards the back of him, he saw movement. A large gray cat. Maybe the smell wasn't cigarette smoke. It could be potpourri or a scented candle. He could see there were no alarm contacts on the windows or glass break sensors. The rug was new with thick padding underneath. Their old chairs were still in the hall.

Ashman moved through the house with his automatic leading the way. When he got to the bedroom, he saw that there were two people in the bed. The man closest to the door, was facing away. He had a large head with dark curly hair. He was a mouth breather. One thick arm was outside the covers. Franca was wearing a nightgown. She used to sleep in flannel pullovers or a big sweat shirt.

Franca awoke as Ashman entered her bedroom with the gun in his hand. She sat bolt upright, furious, her hands over her mouth. She started to scream and then caught it. Ashman could see an expensive watch and ring and that her nails were long. "What?" she half asked and half screamed, her hands clenching into fists.

Ashman silenced her with his finger to his lips, but she screamed out. The large-headed man next to her sat part of the way up. There was a clock radio, a lamp, his glasses, and an ashtray on the night table next to the bed. There was a drawer in the table.

The man started to reach. Ashman closed the distance fast and drove the man's wrist down. When the man's other hand moved, Ashman kicked him in the nose. The man bellowed and blood spurted out.

Franca was screaming, "What do you want? You're crazy. Get out! Get out! " She was bouncing up and down on the bed in her fury.

Ashman turned the gun's black barrel towards her first then to the man, the bedroom door, and the bathroom and back again in a quick smooth arc. Franca covered her mouth with both hands.

The man was yelling, "You're dead You're fucking dead," over and over. He started to reach for his glasses which had been knocked off the night table, but stopped. "You're dead," he said again, holding his bleeding nose.

"Sit back down," Ashman told the bleeding man, who was trying to get free of the covers. "I have your glasses." He swept them up without changing his field of fire. "I'll give them back to you when I go."

The man got up into a sitting position and leaned his head back to stop the nosebleed. His hand and wrist were puffy. He wore a Medic Alert bracelet and appeared to be going into shock.

Franca still had her hands over her mouth, but had gotten out of bed and was walking around and around. Her breasts were showing and she angrily covered them up when she noticed Ashman watching her. "You bastard, you crazy bastard!" she yelled.

"You're fucking dead. I swear it," the man said again through his bloody hands.

Ashman had moved to the corner of the room so he could triangulate them, the bathroom, and the door to the hall. He told Franca to sit down, but she ignored him. He thought about pushing her, but knew not to give up his advantage of distance, even to them. "Be quiet," Ashman said strongly.

"He needs orange juice," Franca told him, "He's diabetic."

"Tell me about Doyle," Ashman said.

"What?" she asked.

"Doyle. He's dead," Ashman answered.

"Dead? Dead, you're dead!" the man yelled.

"Doyle?" Ashman asked again.

"Doyle?" Franca asked. She looked confused and then sad for a moment, but then quickly angry again. "What are you doing in my house?" Franca demanded. "You have no right."

"Into the bathroom, and close the door. Both of you get in the tub," Ashman demanded. "I'll get Romeo here his orange juice and then I'll be out of here in five minutes. No one will get hurt. When I come back from the kitchen, I want you both still in the bathtub with your hands on your heads. In the meantime, keep his head back with pressure on his upper lip. I'll get you ice for his wrist. It's probably broken."

"You're crazy. You're crazy. You always were!" Franca yelled from the bathroom where Ashman had herded them.

"You're dead! You're dead!" the man kept saying, holding his bleeding nose.

Ashman smiled at the nasal-sounding threats as he started down the hall. He came back because they were still yelling and rapped on the bathroom door with the black automatic. "I mean it, Franca," he told her. "I'll be out of here in minutes and everything will be fine. Keep quiet." He paused for a moment and then added slowly, "Or I'll kill you both."

Ashman went into the basement and disabled the phone. There was no alarm, but there was a dedicated line, which he assumed was for a computer. He disconnected it and quickly went through the house looking for the computer to download and anything that could hurt or help him.

There was an empty Mossberg shotgun in the hall closet, pepper gas on Franca's key ring, and a hundred and seventy dollars in their wallets. The man's name was Ray Sabatino. He had a roll of fifties in his pants. There was no computer, but there was a safe in the hall laundry closet. Ashman quickly sprung it. It was empty.

He went into the kitchen and loaded a bag with some fruit, a piece of cheese, a stick of pepperoni, and a container of orange juice. He also took an empty plastic seltzer bottle, which could serve as one shot silencer, and a loaf of bread which could either be a screen against powder burns if he had to shoot them, or his lunch.

Ashman thought about the two of them in the tub. He was sorry about Franca, but it made a funny picture. He wondered who Ray Sabatino was and reminded himself to run his name as he drove away.

Route 209 was a winding road and seemed to go down hill. Ashman weighed his alternatives. He could stay on the outside and gather data, or go back. Ashman smoldered, but knew that the right plan would depend on first getting answers. He would take out whoever was against him the moment that he knew who they were.

Ashman was thinking about candidates for his revenge when he saw the first sign for New York City. He knew he could rest there and see Frankie Valentine, who might help him. The car began to drift, the wheels picking up cinders as he hit the shoulder.

"Shit," he said. Ashman opened all four windows and his shirt so that the cold air would keep him going. He drank some orange juice and bit-off chunks of the pepperoni and cheese. There was a fuel and food stop sixteen miles ahead. Ashman put the radio on and counted the miles as he went.

He went for coffee, confident that the employees would not remember him. The man next to him at the counter wore and old army jacket with a black and yellow First Calvary patch. He saw Ashman notice. "One-Seven," the man announced.

Ashman could see the thousand mile stare in his face. "Rangers, Seventy-fifth," Ashman lied.

"My name is Okie. What's your LZ?" the man asked Ashman. He had the raised scars of a shrapnel wound on the hand he extended.

"Indian Country is my landing zone," Ashman answered.

"I'm driving long haul," the man said. "Jesus riding with me." Okie looked away and back again, "I got Jesus in my heart, but I got Indian Country in my head."

"I hear that," Ashman answered.

When the trucker offered Ashman a lift in his sixteen wheeler, Ashman left Finnegan's car at the rest stop with the keys in it. When he climbed into the rig, there were coffee cups, newspaper comics, and a slicker on the seat. Okie cleared them with a sweep of his arm. "It's safe for democracy now," he said, laughing.

They rode on for awhile and Ashman fell asleep. He woke just before Fort Lee, New Jersey, where they stopped because the bridge had a weight limit. The front wheels of the truck's cab had just crossed onto the bridge when the driver told Ashman, "This is as far as I can go, partner."

"Thanks," Ashman answered. He climbed out and quickly crossed the bridge. The river underneath was thin and dirty. He could see a patrol car go by. A weight violation could cost "One-Seven" his job. Ashman hoped it wouldn't.

He walked across the road and waited for a hitch. Six cars passed him by. Then two teens picked him up, hoping he had some dope. The driver's name was Wade. They were going to the Village. Ashman thought about taking their car, but he let them be and rode in with them, keeping quiet enough to scare them.

He got off at Columbus Circle and walked for a while in

Central Park. Trees helped him get his bearings. Ashman bought a newspaper, a hot dog and a Coke, and walked downtown to the Sheraton. Soon he was sleeping on the floor with one of the twin beds against the door and the other at a right angle to it.

It was morning when Ashman woke up. He went out to get a cab, passing by the ones outside the hotel and over to Fifth Avenue. Two more empty cabs went by. He took the third one after he had walked another block.

The cab took him down Fifth Avenue and around Washington Square. The chess tables were gone. There were Jamaican thugs and crack pushers waiting for business. The place was ugly.

Valentine's Funeral Parlor was on Barrow Street. Ashman remembered the summer he had spent living around the corner on Jane Street. His fourth floor apartment was at the end of the hall and had only one window that overlooked a little courtyard below. He had spent a lot of his time in that courtyard, playing cards and chess on the stone sundial and drinking beer and sangria. Ashman thought about those times as he walked over to Frankie Valentine's.

The funeral parlor was in the middle of the block. Ashman got out of the cab three blocks away to hide his destination. He walked by Valentine's to scope his destination. Then he went up the back alley and came around front. It started to rain.

Before going in, Ashman went over to eat at The Pink Teacup, where he had eaten years ago. It shared a common entrance with a drug store. Both stores still had the bells that rang when someone opened the door. Ashman checked the round clock with the knife and fork hands and looked at the menu posted in the window. Then he went in and sat at the counter.

"No oatmeal, hon," the fat waitress told him. "We got raisin bran, corn flakes, Wheaties, nothin' hot. Waffles, pancakes," she offered. "No French toast."

He took the waffles and an order of toast and bacon. The idea of eggs repulsed him. Ashman felt better after the second cup of coffee. He wondered if the waitress had any memory of him from ten years ago. He had a beard then and with the weight he had lost in the hospital, he was about the same size. She hadn't changed much, but she didn't show a flicker of recognition.

When he was done eating, Ashman walked back around to the funeral parlor. Frankie Valentine was pulling his silver hearse around front so he could put his black BMW in the space in the back. He looked the same, except his hair had more silver in it. Frankie and his mother were both morticians and lived upstairs.

Ashman walked up to the hearse, calling, "Frankie 'V'," as he did.

"Hey," answered Valentine, getting out of the car.

They shook hands and went inside through the waiting room with its high-backed velvet chairs, flocked wallpaper, and serious chandeliers.

As they went down the paneled hall Frankie turned on the sconces. "It looks awfully gloomy without the lights on," he said. They went down the hall and through an ornate door.

Ashman followed the mortician, who talked about how the neighborhood had gone bad, "It's rotten. Them eggplants are ruining everything. I've got clientele who don't want to come down here. You want a drink? We'll have a drink. Then I want to show you my new piece. I picked up a Howda pistol, 16-gauge. Nineteenth Century, 535 grain. They used them to shoot elephants," he said, pointing to a framed woodcut on the wall outside his office. "After I show you to Mother, I'll get the Howda," he went on. "She'll be glad to see you."

They walked by his office and into the next room. An old woman in a violet dress was lying in an ornate box. Valentine put on rubber gloves and began doing her hair. "Look who's here," he said to her.

Ashman knew he'd get no help from Frankie Valentine. Things were getting crazier as they went on, he said to himself. Ashman decided that he was strong enough to go back in and left for a bus to Philly. He'd get the answers there.

Maya

He walked to the Port Authority Bus Terminal to get his endurance back. The beggars and the players were still there. The Nigerians stealing phone numbers were new. There were more Russian thugs. The transit police looked like they were from another planet. Ashman watched the passengers coming and going and the wolves waiting for the weak.

After buying a small bag of popcorn, Ashman boarded his bus early, sitting by the emergency exit and examining everyone who came on board. There were two fat women in flowered dresses that ran together like a sofa. They managed the bus seat by sitting on the edge. A cop in street clothes got on. A young black girl with a silver nose ring sat across the aisle to Ashman's right. The driver was a paunchy white man with thinning red hair, who paid no attention to anything but his newspaper. The bus was equipped with a two-way radio system.

The rest of the passengers got on: two construction workers, a crippled woman, two punks with radios, a man in drag, two nuns, a salesman, and a white woman about forty, who chinked-out her cigarette as she got on board and put the left-over butt in her coat pocket. As the bus was pulling out, a short man with two camera bags got on. He put them under his seat and looked out the window. Ashman cleared a shot at him in his mind, and then at the cop, and then at both of them.

The trip was uneventful except that the punks had foul mouths. The cop told them to "button it," because of the two nuns sitting up ahead. They quieted down after he told them a second time, but they turned their radios up loud until the driver told them to turn it down or he'd stop the bus. Ashman thought of getting up and slapping them.

The bus went out of the yellow fog around New York and down the New Jersey Turnpike to Philadelphia, passing the "Joyce Kilmer" rest stop. Ashman knew who Kilmer was. Doc had told him that when Kilmer was asked why all the poets and the artists went off to World War I to be killed, he had answered, "Because the women were watching." Ashman thought that was as good a reason as any. He would have slept on the bus ride except for the man with the two camera bags.

When Ashman arrived in Philadelphia he bought a newspaper and walked over to Jake's Steaks, passing the antique stores that the street criminals had closed and the ones that dared to stay open to make and sell their old furniture. He had thought about the hot meat and onions at Jake's three or four times since he had been gone.

"What you want, baby, I got it," called Doll Johnson as he

walked in. She kept at her cooking without looking up, scraping the square black grill and squirting on a figure eight of oil. Then she scrambled a wafer of bright red meat with sliced onions. Doll Johnson rocked back and forth while she worked and sang to herself.

"Large, with," Ashman told her through the open take-out window.

"Extry?" she asked.

"Extra," he answered.

"Super extry?"

"Super extry," he told her.

Doll recognized his voice and looked up. "Hey baby," she said. "Where you been?"

"Around and around," he told her.

"I heard that," Doll Johnson answered. She drew a line of sweat off her forehead and slung it on the grill. It went, "psst." "Steam heat, honey," she announced.

She must do that twenty times a day, Ashman thought.

Doll pulled the insides out of a long hard roll and scooped the meat and onions in which she covered with a big enamel spoon of chili. On to that she ladled hot melted cheese and squirted on two lines of ketchup and one of mustard.

Ashman took the hot sandwich and a coffee and went inside to eat. Some of the tables had the chairs upside down. He walked between the rows of them and sat down in line with the take-out window. Ashman ate his sandwich, catching the hot drippings by turning the roll.

While he ate, he watched a mob guy pull up in a three year old Town Car. Two white crack girls walked by with cans of whipped cream in their skeleton hands for five-dollar blow jobs.

Three young blacks wearing black ski hats came to the take-out window. One stood with his back towards the window and two started in. Ashman didn't like the way that looked. He stood up, pushing his chair back.

"It's all right, Baby," Doll said. But Ashman had produced his weapon, racked and ready. He held at his side in plain view.

One of them gestured aggressively. "You bad, fool?" he asked. The second one unzipped his jacket.

Ashman stepped right at them. "I'm Batman," he said as he brought his big automatic up. He was right on top of the them. "Leave or die," he told them. "I'll say it only once."

They turned and left. "We'll be back mutha-fucka," said one of them over his shoulder.

"I'll kill you then," Ashman answered.

"You crazy, Baby," Doll told him, turning back to the grill.

"I dine alone," he answered.

"You crazy, crazy, crazy," she said laughing.

When Ashman was done eating, he walked four blocks up the street to Ronnie Hobbs' Pawn Shop. There were people sleeping on the steam vents on that block, but not in front of Ronnie Hobbs. When they did, somebody from Ronnie's hit them with a bat or squirted them with the hose. A buzzer rang when Ashman opened the door.

"May I help you?" asked one-legged Calvin Lewis through the cage.

Ashman hadn't seen him before. "Is he here?" he asked.

"Is who here?" answered the man behind the cage.

"Ronnie Hobbs. I'm his brother-in-law," Ashman said. That was the code he used to tell the pawn shop owner he was looking to buy or sell a firearm.

Calvin Lewis picked up the phone and went around the corner of the counter with it. He moved from shelf to shelf using his hands and cradling the phone under his chin. Ashman could see he wore a Browning automatic on the side where half his leg was missing.

"Ronnie says to call at six," Lewis said when he swung back around.

Ashman left and walked to the train station, joining the procession of office workers out for lunch and shopping. A man holding ice on his face almost knocked into him, but Ashman felt him coming and moved to the side. Three panhandlers argued over their spot.

Inside the station, two men in red suits buffed the floor from the perimeter in toward the center where the angel of the Memorial to the War Dead went thirty feet to the domed ceiling. She had wings coming down and a fallen man in her arms. Ashman watched the people in the ticket line. He bought his and a cup of coffee which he carried down the ramp.

The train to Bryn Mawr was on time. Only the sofa ladies, who were on the bus with him from New York, and a black nurse with white shoes were on it. The twenty-five minute trip was uneventful.

When Ashman got off, he walked down the arrival steps and across the street. He took the long route, down the big hill and up the two short ones, passing the big homes, most of them Tudor, to the small houses and over to Maya's street on the other side.

* * *

Ashman had first seen Maya Charcot three years ago from the bar window of "The Dirty Glass." She was wearing a black Persian lamb coat. Two men were mugging her and her date. One was trying to get the her date's camel hair coat. She was running in circles around a parked car to avoid the other mugger and came running into the bar for help, screaming and furious at the same time, her hair messed-up from where the mugger had ripped her fur hat off while she was ducking away from him.

Her date was pushing and shoving and holding his own until the one who was chasing Maya went after him. It was getting hairy for him, Ashman remembered, but when Maya came in yelling and crying, six or seven men from the bar, including Dermott, the IRA bartender, went outside to get the bad guys. Ashman followed in the rear.

The bar crowd grabbed the muggers and were going to beat them bad when the one who had been chasing Maya reached inside his coat. Ashman slipped to the front and pinned his hand there. When the other bad guy started to move, Ashman knocked him down. Then he pressed the muzzle of his Charter Arms .44 into the first one's face.

"It was like in the movies," the date said as they calmed down in the bar.

"It probably always is for him," Maya said partially to herself.

The bar patrons toasted each other several times. Maya and her date invited Ashman for a drink to thank him. He sat for awhile and then offered to follow them home which they both appreciated.

Ashman waited outside her apartment after her date left. Her apartment was below street level and had a blue door and blue bars on the windows in the shape of swans. He waited for twenty minutes until she came out to thank him.

Maya told Ashman and that it was all right to leave, which he agreed to do. On her way back in, she wrote her phone number backwards in the condensation on the back window of his car. He waited another twenty minutes down the block.

"You're perfect for me," she told him the night they first made love. "I would have fucked you right there," she told him later. "Up against the bar, our perfect asses inside my Persian lamb coat. You didn't take any shit or give me yours. "Not yet," he told her then, but she pretended not to hear him.

Ashman didn't stay over the first few times they were together. He slept on the floor next to her bed the first night he did, which made Maya feel odd and safe at the same time.

Living in together was complicated. Even two years after he had moved into her house, Ashman kept his own apartment and another place, which was his rotating base camp. He knew if somebody really good wanted to find him, they could, but the triangle he formed between his apartment, his base camp, and Maya's place was enough to distract most, because most weren't very good. It also gave him different angles to get the bad guys if they chose to violate the rule that home was out of bounds.

* * *

Maya's car wasn't there when Ashman got to her house. He went through the small side yard where the white and pink peonies were and into the square back yard. Then he walked around to the front and went in. The alarm was turned off. Ashman armed it and looked through the house. He took four Advils, ate a cheese sandwich and turned the air conditioner on "low" in their bedroom. He slept in the middle room with his guns where he could reach them.

A noise from the kitchen awoke him two hours later. Two voices. He got up and went down the hall, carrying his .40 caliber house gun, which he kept behind his back. The woman's voice was Maya's. He couldn't tell who the other's was, but it was a man's.

Ashman came wide around the corner into the kitchen so he could see the whole room. It was Switt, the skinny physics professor she taught with. He was leaning over Maya's shoulder.

Ashman fired a shot into the stack of Empire dishes on the counter. The sound was deafening. Pieces of the colored dishes exploded through the room, shards of yellow, green and blood, blood red. Switt fell down. The alarm went off. Maya ducked down, covering her ears. Switt started running around and fell. The air was filled with smoke.

Ashman said, "I'm going back to bed." He reset the alarm on his way.

One of the township police officers came to investigate the reports of a gun shot. He parked his cruiser in the front and came up the walk with his hand on his service weapon.

"Microwave accident," Maya told him, shaking her head and laughing a bit.

"Everything all right?" he asked.

"Except my breakfast," she joked. "Sorry," she said. "I'd offer you a cup of coffee, but it's all over the house."

"I bet it is. Be careful," the officer said as he walked back to his car.

Maya went inside. Martin Switt was walking around and around. He looked like his brain wasn't working. Maya called him a cab and cleaned up the kitchen while they waited. She smoked while she cleaned.

Switt, who didn't smoke, asked her for a cigarette and fiddled with it. "He's crazy. He's crazy," he kept saying.

She tried to calm Switt, but by the time Maya walked him to the cab, she was nearly as annoyed with his whining as she was with Ashman. This wasn't the first time Ashman had done such a thing. Once he blackjacked the plumber.

Maya opened all the windows to get the acrid smell out. When Ashman awoke again, she was on the porch dusting her plants and smoking. "Ah, my Ghengis Kahn," she greeted him as he came into the kitchen.

He sat with her at the butcher block table. "Shit," Ashman said, which was the only thing he did say for the next twenty minutes, repeating it two or three times.

He took her car and went out to the store, telling her over his shoulder, "I gotta get some salami."

"Me too," she called, trying to bring him back around.

When Ashman returned, he tossed Maya six chocolate covered cherries one at a time, which was his way of apologizing. Then he cut the salami into thin slices and fried them in an iron pan. They puckered quickly into concave discs. He placed them on white bread, which turned brown with the grease.

Maya filched a slice with a fork and chewed it slowly at the edges as she went out onto the porch again. She was not very good with the plants. They kept dying and she kept replacing them, except for pink and white peonies outside. "Those two are blessed," she always said. "Like us."

Maya stayed outside for a while and then came back in, telling Ashman, "Which reminds me, I brought you something from my conference."

She went to the breakfront and took a small white box from behind the Royal Dalton balloon lady he had bought her at Christmas. Maya gave Ashman the gift with the green ribbon. "It's from the museum in Graz, the one near the clock on the hill. The one that runs backwards. I got it for you on my trip," she told him.

Ashman slid the ribbon off and put it on Maya's finger. He took out the metal soldier. It was finely made.

"Now you can be in two places at once," Maya told him.

Ashman smiled. He put the metal soldier in his shirt pocket and then took it out again and put it on the window sill next to the china balloon lady.

"He belongs here, Ashman told her and went upstairs to sit in a hot tub It was his way of relaxing, turning everything off.

The Invisible Man

Ashman lay in the warm bath water, watching the old sores on his legs pucker up. He thought about how crazy things were as he sat in the tub with a gun in the soap dish. He was not happy that he had shot up Maya's house. It was a crazy thing to do. The world was crazy. People were crazy. Most of it was bad cartoons connected like the tunnels in Nam and the tunnels in the Elms.

Whoever had put him in the hospital had probably killed Doyle and would be coming after him. Usually there was another part which he would figure out, or it would just appear. Which didn't matter Ashman knew, because if he had a chance to stop it, it would be at the last minute, or too late.

He knew you could never tell who was going to try to hurt you. The furrowed scar on his forearm was testament to that. A pregnant woman had tried to cut his throat. That was crazy. Anybody could blow your head off at a thousand yards or your house could have a gas leak. They could stab you in a crowd or poison you in your sleep. That was crazy. Once, some people he knew had sprayed botulism into a crowded room to poison a spy and his cover.

The thing that kept it together for most of the people in his world was field loyalty, foxhole brotherhood, partnering up, going through the shit. Ashman knew if you gave it and got it back, you were lucky. It was the fight, the battle itself, that kept him together, and without it, he'd unravel like the Invisible Man in his bandages. He dreamt of that once, waking up in a cold sweat.

"You were built for rage," Maya had told him, which is why she forgave him for shooting up the kitchen. Ashman knew she was right. It was what had attracted Maya to him in the first place. She once asked him what it felt like. He told her that she couldn't know and didn't want to know what it was like to have your head in Indian Country or Indian Country in your head.

Once Maya saw him kill a man. Ashman told her that he did it because of what the guy had done and what he was going to do, not because of who he was. But she could not forget or forgive. "It was because you saw it," he told her. "Seeing things will make you crazy worse than doing them," Ashman said, but she didn't understand.

Some of the men he knew went crazy because they were still seeing those kinds of things long after they were over. The VA Hospital had rooms of them, who were permanently fucked up and were better off dead, wasting away so slow, so long, that their families had long since stopped coming to see them. Two patients down the hall from Doyle's uncle had been at the V.A.

Hospital since World War II. Both had their legs blown off and one of them was left blind during the week of their nineteenth birthdays, more than fifty years ago.

Some of those who had gone crazy were still working "at the craft." They were still working in the espionage trade because crazy as they were, they were still good at what they did. Cupid Burroughs was like that from the seizures he had gotten from his third skull fracture. He was taking his Dilantin and watching it ruin his teeth as he waited for the next blow that would kill him. "No problem," he told Ashman and Doc when they saw him last. "I'm always walking backward so nobody can sneak up on me."

"We're all like milk cartons," Doc answered, "We're going merrily along with expiration dates stamped on our heads."

The secret was to get out in time and have a real life, which is what Eggs Doyle had done. Doyle's last job was at National Executive Services with Lorraine Knoddles. Knoddles was good. She had active military and Secret Service experience.

They were working a man named Carroll, who was trying to buy jet bomber parts for the Saudis. Carroll liked young boys. Knoddles was sitting in Carroll's living room when one of his men came in with a kid over his shoulder in a blanket. Knoddles thought it was a boy about six or seven.

Doyle walked in as Carroll pulled the blanket back and licked the kid's butt cheek. "Good eatin'," Carroll told the guy carrying the boy. Doyle shot them both. He shot Carroll in the face and his man twice in the chest in one smooth arc. The .45 rounds blew away Carroll's head and knocked the other one across the room with a gaping hole in him.

There would have been hell for Doyle to pay, but Knoddles covered for him. They carried the kid out in the blanket and took him to St. Vincent's Hospital. And that was it for Doyle. He bought the bar, "Kelly's Sure Thing", and stayed there with his wife and had an everyday life.

After he had retired, Doyle said what he missed most was the brotherhood, not the service or the shit. He tried to get them all together every spring. They drove down to Florida with their cars filled with shotguns, counting road kill. When they got to Boca or Disneyworld, they walked around drunk on vodka and beers. Cupid Burroughs eventually moved there and ran a restaurant until he died. Prinzi drove a school bus in Boca Raton and played trumpet on Saturday nights.

Ashman wouldn't take that Florida trip with them, although he met them there once. He didn't feel safe with them all there together. "Like shooting sharks in a barrel," he tried to explain, but Doyle said he was crazy. He often thought of that conversation. "They're going to come to kill you one day, Eggs," Ashman had told him, "They always do."

"Who's they?" Doyle asked.

"The one's you don't kill first," Ashman answered. Doyle laughed and shook his head.

* * *

Ashman got out of the tub and dried off. He still had the twenty-five year old fungus infection on his legs, and he toweled that last, applying another medicated cream. He walked down the hall, and tossed his towel in the hamper. Maya knew to soak the towels in bleach so she didn't get "the oozing rot," as he called it. Ashman poured himself a beer, which he drank in the nude, and feel asleep after reading the mail.

He dreamt like he often did since the war. Sometimes those dreams went away for a while, but they always came back. They were running, jumping, crying, burning, bleeding, dreams; awful and without end or hope.

When Ashman got to Vietnam he was told those dreams would be coming. Somebody had called them the "Incomin'-outgoin'-shit kickin'-heart breakin' cowboysuit wearin'-mama cryin'-choir singin'-first kiss-I got you by the balls-puckered asshole-help me sweet Jesus-no answer-nobody's home blues dreams.

Now those war dreams came with dreams about his imprisonment in the hospital and about Doyle being dead. They went on together, like the tunnels in Vietnam and the tunnels under the Elms. Ashman knew that when he had avenged Doyle's death and gotten those who had put him in the Elms Hospital, those new dreams would stop. "Retaliation is the best cure for nightmares," was one of Doyle's favorite sayings.

* * *

The next morning Ashman went to his basecamp. There was a message from Knoddles on his answering machine. She had left it for him in the agreed upon fashion, "I'm sorry. I have the wrong number. I wanted to talk to Art."

"Yo, partner," she answered when Ashman called her back.

They decided to meet for lunch, talking sideways since they were on the phone and they knew that no phones were secure. When he hung up, Ashman wondered if Knoddles had taken him down. Anesthesia or nerve poison probably put him in the hospital, maybe curare or resperine. Knoddles once took a target out by painting his hairbrush with curare.

It was not unheard of to be taken out by one of your own. Two years ago three guys he had worked with were taken out in New Mexico. The story was that they were into unsanctioned activity, and rogue behavior wasn't tolerated. Ashman heard that Dakkas was asked to go get them, but then he heard an ex-SEAL from out West handled the job because Dakkas got the chicken pox. The rogues were blown into chili.

Ashman drove to New York and met Knoddles at Fibonacci's. There was a new iron railing outside of the restaurant to keep the crowds from pushing themselves down the steps and through the front window. He got there fifteen minutes early. It was raining and nobody was outside.

Knoddles looked good and was glad to see him. There was a bond between them, not only because they had been at risk together and watched each other's back, but because Ashman never made a thing about her lesbianism. "I don't care what kind of balls you have, Lorraine," he had told her, "You put them on the line."

They kissed when they met which is what they all did. It was started by the Italians in their group because their fathers kissed their grandfathers. Cupid Burroughs, who was black, wouldn't kiss anybody, but had learned to take a kiss on the cheek after being told that Sicily was in Africa.

Knoddles kissed Ashman on the mouth. "You look great, Sport," she said, "but you could use a vacation." That meant she thought he looked like shit.

"That bad?" he laughed. "Low-rain," he said slowly and squeezed her hand.

The waitress came over, a tall blonde in her thirties. She looked at Ashman and then at Lorraine like she knew them. "Would you like something to drink before you order?" she asked.

Knoddles had Jack Daniels on the rocks and Ashman had Crown Royal up. They ate chicken cacciatore and dunked their bread in the red gravy. She poked at her spinach and garlic, taking little bits at a time, trying to accommodate her hiatal hernia and the gas that would kill her later. They had coffee and apple pie. When the bill came, they split it.

Lorraine put her arm through his. "Let's walk and talk," she said.

They went up the block in the wrong direction for two blocks to walk off their dinner, passing by Emilio's where they had sat for hours years before with Doc and Doyle.

"Good times," she said.

"The best," he answered.

They walked back up Seventh Avenue and over to Perry Street. There was an alley between them and her car. As they crossed, Knoddles saw two bad guys. "Ten o'clock," she told Ashman. She cross-drew her Glock from inside her blazer. "I got right."

A third man, Hispanic, burly, got out of his car on their left. "Don't move!" said Ashman. as he closed on him quickly, taking back their flank. When the man twitched, Ashman knocked him down and out, going behind him so he could keep his sight line on the others. As he did, he heard Knoddles call, "Mac 10!"

Ashman took cover behind the front bumper of the Hispanic's blue Ford and cleared his field of fire. Left to right, he thought. He had Golden Saber rounds in his weapon. Even thought his ammo was hot, Ashman looked for head shots because he knew that if the enemy had automatic weapons, they probably were wearing armor. He'd take lower body too. No civilians, no windows. Knoddles had gone two cars down so they had the alley pinched up. The fat Hispanic was down in the gutter.

They had good cover and were combat ready and waited in position a long time. Nothing happened. Then Ashman signaled an 'all clear'. The enemy was gone. The Hispanic was sitting against a car in a stupor and had puked on himself.

Knoddles came out from behind her cover. "Coming left," she called.

Ashman came out, going the long way around to extend their perimeter. Knoddles smiled when they hooked up again. "Shazam!" she said. "This shit gets my blood pumping."

"Thank heaven for little things," he laughed.

They talked about who the bad guys were. "I think the third guy was just passing by," Ashman said.

"Wrong place, wrong time," Knoddles answered. "Same difference."

After they drove around for a while in Knoddles' Jeep, she told him why she had called. She had a job upcoming, which was bad because she was in her sister's wedding in Atlanta.

Knoddles gave him some preliminary details and when Ashman said yes, she gave him the rest of it.

Knoddles gave him a photo to study and the itinerary, as well as an airline ticket. She also gave Ashman a business-size manila envelope that held a thin, hard, plastic knife with a four-inch blade. She'd pay him when she got paid, which was fine with Ashman. The job was clean and cleared. And she told him if he didn't use the airline ticket, he could keep the refund if he found a way to do that clean.

Even though Ashman knew that Lorraine's work was reliable and that her diagram of the airport would be good, he decided to reconnoiter for himself. He'd go over her route and his alternates. Ashman visualized the killing field and the various scenarios in his head and asked her the right questions. He would use his own weapon.

* * *

When the time for Knoddles' job came, Ashman was there early at O'Hare's Departure Gate 35B. Fulliard Stevens looked just like the photo Knoddles had given him, Andover, Amherst, and Harvard. He was an athletic, smart-looking black man with a gray suit, white shirt and club tie. Not a mark, stain, or wrinkle on him. Ashman waited until Stevens passed through the metal detector at the airport: Cartier watch, college ring, keys, a cell phone, and beeper.

Ashman went through with his props: Timex watch, keys with a Celtics key ring, a bronchial inhaler. As the passengers started to board, he positioned himself between an elderly white woman behind Stevens and two college girls. With the line moving forward toward the plane, Ashman slid his left leg ahead six inches and hooked the old lady.

They both went down and one of the girls behind tripped over them. Ashman reached out like he was trying to catch the old woman. He slid his right arm under hers, driving his hard plastic knife into Stevens' leg. He tore up and over with the blade, severing the femoral artery. As Stevens fell, Ashman stabbed him in the heart.

There was scrambling, screaming, and spurting blood. In the confusion, Ashman took off his bloody jacket and walked quickly to the left into a crowd of arriving passengers. A soft hat and glasses on a red string were a quick change of costume and with his jacket off, the only remarkable thing about his appearance was the bright yellow shirt which was not visible before.

After the job, Ashman went back to Maya's. She was grading mid-terms. It was a good time for the two of them with Maya off for semester break. They did some day trips, the Inner Harbor in Baltimore and the outlets in Reading. She bought him some Eddie Bauer things.

"You dress like a pauper," she told him. Ashman didn't bother much about clothes except for work, but he liked lamb's wool sweaters and he couldn't wear socks with tight elastic. They went to the movies twice and spent Saturday in bed.

Major Coates

Retired Marine Major Kyle Lee Coates had onyx eyes and huge hands. His experience behind the fence and outside the wire made him the perfect Director of the Pentagon's Advanced Research Project Agency.

Coates chief responsibility was Non-Lethal Weapons. He had watched numerous demonstrations of NLW's, including microwave guns, light beam rifles, and soundwave weapons. He had even reviewed bizarre proposals for the application of mind power and the new physics, including astral projection, clairvoyance, and telepathy.

The Major knew that while there had always been tinkering in weaponeering, the growing interest in non-lethal weapons had created a burgeoning industry outside of the government. Controlled by an odd combination of wierdo leftists and budget obsessed right wingers, this group of weaponeers made the Pentagon very nervous. This was particularly true when the kitchen-made weapons were viable. The Israeli's for instance, were field testing hand-held, light weapons based upon plans originating from a group of Harvard wonks. Similarly, a NLW originated by hackers at Berkeley, was being tested by the Japanese.

It was centralization that the Pentagon wanted, not the decentralization which the NLW's fostered. The Major's superior, General E. Edward Kendall, had told him more than once, "Imagine that a sea of interloping egghead technoids develop the next stealth technique. We'd have chaos and chaos is not a healthy thingfor the good guys."

Coates respected General Kendall, but he did not like being inside ARPA's Pentagon headquarters. He was underground with no windows and had to suffer the continuous backwash from competing agencies such as the FBI, CIA and the National Justice Institute. Inside work, with its politics and inter-agency competition, allowed the Major little leeway. He hated it like he hated his windowless office.

Field work kept the Major alive. He was authorized by General Kendall to run the operation projects essentially as he wished, subject only to the Agency's general guidelines and the General's occasional directions. Major Coates was permitted for instance, to select non-agency personnel from an approved outside list. It was felt that using Pentagon personnel for the investigation and interdiction of what might be otherwise legitimate activity by legitimate citizens, could lead to substantial public relations problems.

This

approved outside list was composed of personnel who had already retired or were on some kind of early-out from one appropriate government service or another. What made these people particularly valuable was that they still had their contacts and loyalty. They also usually had one or more pensions to protect, which is why they were referred to as "double dippers," or more often, "dippers."

By any standard the "dippers" were better than the Mafia or mercenaries. They certainly were more reliable than the dozen or so crazies who were kept "on the reservation," for kamikaze missions. Only six months before, the Major had to eliminate one of the kamikazes, who had decided to take his own view of the world to its logical extreme, which in his mind, meant killing Michael Jordan and poisoning the New York water supply.

All of the updated data on the "dippers" was available to the Major at a touch of a button. By access to his universe of knowledge, he could tell who was fading and who was still serviceable. He also had the "dippers" in for regular evaluations and had their work monitored, not only for quality control, but as a means of checks and balances.

Major Coates' most recent field operation involved a "sound to light" or sonnoluminescence NLW. There had been attempts to convert sound to light for industrial and military use for almost fifty years. Despite the great energy potential however, none of these projects had reached fruition. Most recently, a sonnoluminescence project had been started and then dropped by the Navy Department and then pursued and also discontinued by the Illinois Institute of Technology.

The sonnoluminescence field project assigned to Major Coates appeared to be distinctive primarily because of an apparent coincidence; one of his dippers was living with one of the project's scientists, Maya Charcot. The Major wondered if this was the primary reason that General Kendall had given him the assignment, but knew not to question the assigned task.

Coates knew that his plan had to be more complex than usual because of the coincidence. He created a detailed blueprint for dealing with the sonnoluminescence weapons and addressed several contingencies and an increased number of checks and balances. He himself would make contact with the NLW group that evening. As suggested by the General, Lorraine Knoddles had already been sent on an interdiction assignment.

* * *

The only people Major Kyle Lee Coates spoke to at The Republic Club that afternoon, other than the doorman, were the barber and the bartender. The Major came in the side door as he always did and followed the blue carpet to the left and down the wide stairs to the barber shop on the lower level. The club afforded him quiet and he used that to review his plans and systems, as well as to unwind.

"Porch monkeys," Joe Anastasia, the barber, said.

The Major was thinking about the sound-to-light project under the hot towel wrapped around his face and didn't answer.

"It's a sin, them eggplants," the barber went on. "If it wasn't for the welfare, they'd be at our throats, them coconuts, confusing kindness for weakness the way they do."

Anastasia shaved the Major, pulling his skin tight with his

left hand and wiping the lather on to the paper towel next to him. When he was done with the shave, the barber splashed witch hazel on his hands and patted it on the Major's face. Then he massaged in a layer of pink cream to close his pores.

Coates sat up slowly. Anastasia took a vibrating hand unit and massaged his scalp and neck. When he was done, the barber brushed his jacket off. The Major signed his bill and tipped him.

"Next Tuesday, Major?" the barber asked.

"I'll have to call you, Joseph," the Major answered. He went upstairs for a Boodles and tonic.

The Republic Club's bartender, Dan Maloney, worked forty minute shifts, which is how long his bladder and kidneys could wait. "Hazards of 'the job', Your Honor," he told the Major as he went for his second piss in the last hour.

He had been a thirty year wagon man for the Eighth District and the jostling of the patrol wagon and the sea of bad coffee had taken their toll. "Sometimes my pee just falls out, like Jell-O," Maloney continued as he poured a second gin. The Major drank half and started a cigar, giving one to the bartender, who sniffed it and put it under the counter.

"Thank you, Your Honor," the bartender said. "I'll have it after my shift."

Major Coates nodded and went upstairs to the sitting room to review his strategies for that evening's meeting with the NLW group.

* * *

While Coates was sipping his drink, Professor Maya Charcot was doing her hair. Even though Maya wore her hair cut short, she paid a lot of attention to it. She wanted a professional, yet stylish look when she met with Major Coates, who she thought was Bruce Hackett, a government procurement officer.

Maya went over the notes she had spread out on her vanity. Dr. Switt would be at the meeting, as well as their minority partner, Fulliard Stevens, who was flying in from Chicago. Attorney Martin Greenglass, Switt's brother-in-law, had set up the meeting and would arrive twenty minutes early to review their preparation.

Dr. Charcot had presented a paper on sonnoluminescence four years before at Boston University. She was now working with Switt in pursuing practical applications of the sound-to-light theory as a means of getting their university grant extended. Maya thought about starting that evening's presentation with a line she used when she first presented her paper at Boston U., "Two priests and a physicist were in a boat..."

It started raining as the Major left the club for his dinner meeting. He lowered his head to keep the end of the cigar from getting wet as he walked from the club and he was glad that his car was nearby.

Major Coates arrived twenty minutes late so that he could control the group with his entrance. They were sitting in a small private dining room off to the left. The lawyer was talking and pointing. The Major sat down as his drink arrived. Greenglass did the introductions. The waitress came over and they ordered dinner. Coates let the lawyer continue his soliloquy.

The group thought Major Coates was the Federal

Administrative Contracting Officer looking for a free meal, and maybe more. The lawyer clearly controlled them.

Greenglass went on about how much he knew about government contracting and how righteous he was, "We will meet all Department of Defense Form 1707 requirements and nothing we do will run afoul of any Federal Acquisition Regulations, including but not limited to regulations Three, Seven or Twelve."

"And Regulation Four?" asked the Major, referring to the anti-contingency fee provision of the Federal Acquisition Regulations.

Greenglass laughed in self-defense. The meal came. The Major and Greenglass ate veal chops. The other two had pasta and salad.

While they were still eating, the Major asked for their presentation. "If you have anything else for me, could you do it now," he said. "I do have another meeting."

Switt was able to explain the process well enough, except that his hands shook terribly when he spoke. Sonnolumenescence, he explained, was a means of converting sound into light by imploding the walls of pressurized air bubbles with sound waves. Switt contended that the application of modern optical technology could generate powerful laser-quality bursts suitable for industry or the military.

"Very Old Testament," said Maya, which was the little joke she settled on.

Major Coates, who was watching her lips move, laughed, but Greenglass didn't. Then the Major told the NLW group that the reason he was there was to explain "Small Disadvantaged Business." He pointed out that the continued absence of their African-American partner, Mr. Stevens, would disqualify them as SDB.

He paused and went on to draw them out, "You'll probably need three hundred and fifty thousand dollars up front; for salaries, lab time, patent work, a prototype and something off the top for legal fees."

"No, actually...," Switt started, but Greenglass cut him off, "I can tell you right now, we won't give up a piece for Research and Development," the lawyer said. "And salaries aren't a proble. We wouldn't be wasting everybody's time without a prototype. We've done our R and D."

The lawyer nodded to Switt, who brought a large briefcase from under the table. Inside was a portable video player. Major Coates stood so that no passersby could see the presentation.

It was a standard industrial demonstration conducted inside what appeared to be a university laboratory. There were two people present. Both were wearing eye shields, but it was clear to the Major that they were Switt and Dr. Charcot.

A glass cylinder approximately three feet in length and two feet in diameter was mounted into a metal frame. At one end ran a thick electrical cord. At the other end was a bracket in which the man placed a thick glass lens.

"The Holographic Optical Element," Switt told Major Coates. "It's our little "'hoe,'" he almost giggled.

The camera panned from the canister to a piece of aluminum and back again. Within minutes bubbles began to appear in the cylinder. They increased and coursed through the glass cylinder which could be seen to vibrate. After approximately three minutes, a beam of blue-white light emitted through the optical lens. It burned a neat hole through the metal target a dozen feet away.

The Major acted annoyed.

"You understand, Mr. Hackett, that this was just a …," started Greenglass.

"Parlor trick, counselor? I came here to provide you with information, not to watch your home movies."

Major Coates had been convinced by the demonstration that the technology of the Non-Lethal Weapon had potential. This particular NLW group, however, was composed of amateurs. Their performance reminded him of the World War II fiasco in which a bathtub demonstration convinced the Navy Department to embark on a plan to flatten Okinawa with a tidal wave. He would see that a similar mistake did not occur with this project.

"I have another appointment," he said. "I'm sure Attorney Greenglass will know what to do next. By the way," the Major added, "Who shot your video?"

"We took it auto timer and what not," Switt answered. "Was it alright?"

Coates got up. He was intrigued by the woman and looked forward to investigating her. He touched Maya's shoulder as he left.

Greenglass did most of the talking while his group waited another forty-five minutes for Fulliard Stevens, who lay bleeding to death at O'Hare Airport. When their minority partner did not arrive, they went their separate ways.

Maya left for her little vacation with Ashman. Her plan was to get to the hotel, change into her sweats, and take a run around the lake before he arrived. She had packed good lotion to protect her skin against the chafe of the wind. She'd have a hot bath after.

Killings

When Lorraine Knoddles returned from her sister's wedding, she called Ashman at his basecamp. He called her back. "Everything's fine," he told her.

"Good. That's nice," she answered. "You want to come for dinner on Friday?"

"Let's go out. Chinese good?"

Lorraine told him that was fine. She understood that while he was not critical of her personal life, he wasn't comfortable being around Mina Shaw.

Knoddles had seen to it that the Fulliard Stevens job was properly closed. She was paid for it and brought cash to her dinner with Ashman. Lorraine put the envelope inside her newspaper. With it was confirmation of the airfare and hotel reservations that Lorraine had made for Ashman's vacation.

"One of the remaining perks from NES," Lorraine told Ashman when she passed over the paper. "The imperialistic, capitalist conglomerate which now owns National Executive Services still gives me discounts at the New Conquistador Hotel, which they also own." Ashman thanked her. "Don't bite me or Mina," she said laughing, "but we'll being staying there too."

"As long as we don't have to have dinner together," Ashman answered, smiling. "Besides, you know I'm jealous."

They had a nice time together, and hugged good-bye.

"Sorry there's no gun-play this time, Lorraine," Ashman told her.

"Me too," she answered.

Lorraine Knoddles looked forward to the relaxed weekend. The wedding in Atlanta had been annoying. Twice she was asked about when she was going to be married. As far as she was concerned, she was.

Lorraine and Mina arrived at the hotel together.

"I got to take a run," Mina told her after they checked in. "I'll jog around the lake."

"I'll stretch out for a couple of minutes," Knoddles said, "and then start a hot bath for you."

"Love ya," Mina said as she left.

"Me too." Lorraine answered. She looked out the window, hoping she could see Mina on her run around the lake that lay in the night like a silk robe.

Ashman drove in from the airport. He was not very good at vacations, but he looked forward to seeing Maya, who was waiting for him.

Inside the hotel, a sweet love was waiting for her rendezvous. She bent, pink and nude and poured her bath salts that shimmered like pearls into the warm waiting water. The bath shone pink like the walls around it and then flashed and roared the air with hurling red fire, black smoke, white porcelain axes, and knife shards of pastel tiles.

Maya and Mina had been running around the night lake in opposite directions, towards the lake wind and away from it, crossing each other's paths and the wind that blew across the lake, running towards the waiting warmth and their love. Then they ran harder and weaker, falling as they ran, but going on, pulled down and towards their rooms and Lorraine Knoddles who exploded into the night sky.

There were flashing lights and ladders reaching up. Firemen in black suits and yellow boots were coming down to white stretchers and red and blue trucks and police that looked like they came from outer space. There were flashing lights, smoke, and howling noises, clanging noises, babbling noises, and screaming.

When Mina saw the room blown out, she knew Lorraine was dead. Mina fell down, rolling on the ground for the loss that opened and had no end. Mina knew she would never be the same. Never, ever. Mina had lost her sister, her armor, and her love and now would forever hear the clanging noises and smell the burning and see the black night turned flashing red.

Ashman watched the commotion and the destruction, counting the windows up from the ground and down from the top to see that it wasn't Maya's room, his room, her, who had been torn to pieces, and he wondered whether there was a mezzanine to count. He saw Maya walking up, turning in little circles as she did, her hands on her head like a surrendering prisoner. She was making crying sounds, and she looked lost. Maya was crying about her plants, "It's a big mess. It's a big mess," she said over and over.

"You're safe. You're safe," Ashman told her. When he took Maya to his car, he saw that she had wet herself. She was still crying and made no sense. He thought about where to take her. Ashman drove away, his windshield wipers cleaning off the fallen broken things and the little pieces of horrid, smoking jelly.

He drove out to the four lane street and onto the interstate highway. There was an Emergency Services Unit van ahead of them on the right about a hundred yards. As Ashman approached it, he thought he saw its front left tire begin to change lanes. There was a gray Ford ahead of him in his lane. The Ford was dirty and the chrome was pitted. It began to slow down and Ashman had to break.

The ESU van slowed and then came even with him. Ashman could see the two Stevens 12 gauge shot guns ready in their rack. He slid his .45 out from under his right thigh and cleared the safety, keeping it at his right hand, but away from Maya's sight or reach. "Spray and pray," he said to himself about the shotguns.

Maya could partially hear him over the radio he had put on for her. "What?" she asked, looking out the window.

Ashman didn't answer. He was getting ready for war.

The van drove off and the Ford pulled away. Ashman turned the radio up. They drove for another hour and stopped for coffee. Maya had two cups of coffee and smoked a half-dozen cigarettes, leaving one or two of them still burning. She calmed down as they drove on and wanted to talk about what had happened.

"What, is it me?" she asked. "Did anybody get killed? Did it have something to do with me? After all," she said finally, "we're making that thing."

Ashman lost his patience. "Jesus, Maya," he told her. "It's not the fucking Manhattan Project you're working on. What you're doing is lab stuff. If anybody thought what you were doing was important enough, they'd wait until you had something worthwhile and then they'd steal it, not kill you. Maybe the hotel explosion was a gas leak or maybe the Iraqi, or those fertilizer patriots or the ghost of Christmas Past. Maybe an insane textile salesman. You're safe. You're safe. Let's find a place to drink some gin and take a swim. Everything will be fine. It is fine. Maybe we'll find a good Italian restaurant. Chicken cacciatore? Think about that."

Maya said, "Yes." She felt better knowing Ashman wasn't worried. Maybe they would have a vacation after all. She curled up and wrapped her feet in his jacket that he had put over her to keep her warm.

As they drove on, the Ford appeared again, coming up on them from behind with the lights flashing in its grill. Ashman knew that he was speeding, so he slowed. He put the .45 back under his right thigh and pulled to the shoulder of the road.

The Ford came up behind, but far enough back to pull around if it had to. The Emergency Services Unit with the shotguns was nowhere in sight. Ashman waited with battle contingencies in his mind.

There were two men inside the car. The swarthy one got out and walked up to Ashman with his badge out. The other was on the radio. Ashman could see that the one coming up wore cheap clothes and cop's shoes. He looked like a plainclothes, except the walk didn't look quite right.

"Stay in your vehicle, please," the swarthy one told them. He approached Ashman's vehicle holding up his shield. He was wearing a Smith and Wesson Model .49 and looked tired. "Can I see your license, registration and proof of insurance?" he asked.

Ashman showed him an impeccable, but phony Cleveland Police I.D. along with his license.

The cop, whose name was Tarkanian, looked tired and was glad to accept the badge. He had that "too many shifts for too many days" look. He talked about what was going on, the other plainclothes still hanging back in the Ford and smoking. "We don't know whether we're in the shit or it's a gas leak," Tarkanian said. "But you were coming from the scene pretty f-ing fast. My partner, Steyr's dad, was 'on the job' in Cleveland," he went on, "Maybe he'll want to say 'yo.'"

Tarkanian walked back to his partner, who was leaning against the Ford. Steyr came over. He walked like a cop. He was big and freckled and had his sleeves rolled up. Ashman couldn't see a side-arm. He was probably wearing a pancake holster in the back.

The two cops passed each other on the way. Steyr took a cigarette from his shirt pocket and threw it to his partner, who lit up and smoked, while Ashman and Steyr bullshitted for a couple of minutes about "the job" and Cleveland and the fucking Cleveland Browns and how they should rot in hell.

Steyr wished him a safe trip. Tarkanian was up ahead by the Ford and Steyr was walking back when Ashman saw him start to step across with his right foot. His right arm was moving to his holster.

Ashman hit his horn and slammed his car into reverse. "Down! Get down!" he told Maya, reaching over to push her. As Steyr pivoted with his gun out, Ashman fired four shots. One shot was high and missed, but the others were good, hitting the target in the thigh, chest, and throat. Steyr got two rounds off. One narrowly missed Maya.

Tarkanian was pounding out shots as Ashman drove at him full speed ahead. Tarkanian emptied his revolver and was speedloading as he ran bowlegged for the cover of the Ford. Ashman ran him down and shot him dead.

Maya was screaming, and their windshield was shot out. She was throwing herself around, and her forehead was bleeding from glass splinters. She was shivering. Ashman tried to calm her but she went on. "Home, home. Take me home," Maya said over and over.

"We're going home now," Ashman told her. He took her to the Ford because their windshield was gone. Maya tried to pull away. Ashman grabbed her by the wrist and brought her to him in a 'come-along' lock.

Her eyes were wide as they drove away. She was rocking back and forth. Ashman listened to the car's scanner while Maya smoked Steyr's cigarettes. Maya thought she was back home and going on a trip.

Ashman knew the Ford wasn't right. He knew that someone was coming after him and that he had to put Maya somewhere . Then he could either disappear or go for the enemy's heart, wherever that was. He wanted to take her home, but Ashman knew that whoever they were could just as easily let her go, triangulate for him, and slit her throat later.

He thought about leaving Maya in front of the Liberty Bell. He would find himself a high tree like he had in-country in Nam, in so far he was behind everybody, living in the crooks of branches, drinking the rain. He'd climb down and go rushing through the tunnels to come up and kill the enemy in their sleep. Ashman had the radio all the way up and Maya was rocking back and forth. He felt the rush of battle and was glad for it.

They passed four more highway exits. Ashman turned off at the fifth. He found a motel and checked in. There was a package store across the road and Ashman got tonic, ice, and Blue Sapphire gin. They sat together on the tan sofa next to the bed. She leaned against him and talked and smoked and drank gin until she fell asleep. He took a quick shower with the bathroom door open.

Two hours later, Ashman took her out to the SUV he had stolen. As they drove off, he told her they were going for a swim. Maya fell asleep, dreaming of them sitting in the waves.

Ghosts

Ashman thought about it all as he drove on with Maya. He wondered whether the hotel explosion was meant for her. If so, it would be because of her physics project. That was a long-shot, he told himself, since the project was elementary and the explosion was so large, so clumsy. The explosion might have been aimed at someone else, but he didn't believe in coincidence. It was more likely that someone was still after him.

He thought about Franca, how Franca and him had been together. She had wanted him out before he left eight years ago, even when they were still sitting outside on the glider, watching the night. He remembered his desire to kill the man in her bed and how angry she was. Then Ashman wondered why he thought about her at all.

They drove through the night, stopping only to use the bathroom or get food which they ate in the car. Ashman used evasive tactics and was reasonably sure that he wasn't followed, particularly because he had switched vehicles again. He drove by their exit on the turnpike and stopped at the next rest stop.

There was a bank of pay phones in the well-lit parking lot. Ashman knew that although pay phones were safe from everybody on the outside, he must assume that his enemy would be privy to any telephone conversation. He called Stevie Venudo's beeper and punched in "345," for emergency, half of sixty-nine, meaning he was in a position to have it bitten off. Stevie called him back in thirty seconds. He was reliable and loyal to Ashman ever since they had met at the pistol range ten years ago.

Detective Steve Venudo was loyal because of Ashman's convincing lies about having been on the Cleveland Police Department. Loyal was the way Venudo and his police friends treated "good guys" who had been "on the job." It was their code. Ashman valued their relationship because of that code and because it helped him in what he did.

"You all right?" Venudo asked him when he called back.

"Yeah, Stevie. It's party time. I need you to carry something to the farm. Don't be shy."

"I hear ya. You all right," he asked again.

"I'm all right," Ashman answered. "It's party time."

Ashman had directed Stevie to go to Maya's and take her to Rosie's. Rosie's block was safe. A cop and a retired cop lived on the block and a church was in the back. Also, old man Gigante, the aged Mafioso, had been buying his groceries there for years, which made Rosie's off limits to the local criminals.

Ashman let Maya out in front of her house. Venudo was there. For a moment, Maya thought he there to hurt her. She felt the bottom fall out when Ashman drove away and her knees buckled.

Then she noticed the gold shield on the man's blue suit and thought the police had come for Ashman. That had happened once before. Maya thought about running into the house or back to the car. Her heart raced.

"Dr. Charcot?" Venudo asked. He bent over to pick up the newspaper in the driveway. "I'm a friend of Ashman," he told her. "A good friend. Don't worry."

Maya was still shaken. She reached her hand out for the newspaper. Venudo misunderstood and shook hands with her. Maya laughed nervously.

"What do you want?" Maya asked. She fidgeted with the pocketbook which hung from her shoulder.

Venudo saw her lingering fear. "Ashman sent me," he told her. "He asked that I look after you while he's away a couple of days. He said to tell you that you wrote your phone number backwards on the back window of his car, 232-7654, and that you'd know everything was all right by me knowing that." He moved towards her slowly, herding her towards the front door.

"We were away," Maya said. She had one hand on the white railing and still held on to her bag with the other.

"We'll talk inside." Venudo thought that she looked sexy and a little bit crazy.

"Do you have the keypad to disconnect the alarm," he asked. "I have the code. He gave it to me. 6-1-5-8-5."

It calmed her that he knew it. She leaned against the little white railing and opened her bag. Venudo watched her carefully and shifted a bit so he could reach his .357, but saw her take a cigarette.

"Don't you carry one on your keys?"

Maya was confused, but remembered that there was a key pad for her alarm on the ring with her car keys. "It's on the car thing. I never use it." She gave it to Venudo, still holding the unlit cigarette in her hand. "Sorry," she said, waving the cigarette which she switched into her other hand. She lit it, double inhaling the smoke, and turning away from him to exhale.

The detective went in first and checked her house. Maya had a half dozen questions, but Venudo told her to pack quickly. Rosie Mastrangelo came in. She was in uniform, but had her hair in a pony tail. The way it bounced when she walked reminded Maya of a cheerleader.

Rosie could see that Maya was upset. "You're goin' to stay at my house for a while," she said, adding, "It'll be like a pajama party. I'll help you pack."

The wallpaper was drawings of flowering plants and Rosie admired it. "It looks like a garden," she added.

"They're the only plants I don't kill," Maya answered with half a joke. "Is he all right?" she asked Rosie, without turning around. "Ashman, is he alright?"

"He's fine," Rosie told her at the top of the stairs.

There were two bedrooms off the hall and a study. Maya's clothes were in the middle room. Rosie stood outside while she packed her suitcases and a make-up bag. "Am I over doing it? The packing, I mean?" Maya asked.

"It'll only be a couple of days, hon," Rosie answered.

Maya didn't seem to listen and packed another little bag.

When they came downstairs, AL Couington was standing in the doorway. He startled Maya. Couington was 6'6" and, with his reddish afro, he looked like a giant. Venudo and Rosie acted as if he was expected, so Maya said nothing. They took Maya to the car which Rosie had pulled up on the lawn right outside of her front door.

Venudo got in his car and flashed the lights. He led their three cars up on to the Expressway with Rosie and Maya in the middle and Couington, who had parked up the block, bringing up the rear. They stayed in the right lane and got off at Oregon Avenue.

Twice, cars tried to pull into the right lane which would have separated the convoy, but Venudo slowed up and Couington accelerated . They rode bumper to bumper for almost a mile. The rest of the trip was uneventful except for a city trash truck that tried to pull out between them. The driver honked his horn and yelled out for them all to kiss his fat ass.

Frankie Cigars

Rosie's neighborhood had shrunk to a six block by six block area, but it looked after itself. A block over were the Asians, or "the Chinee," as the neighborhood called them. They were mostly Laotians and Cambodians, and some new Vietnamese. They lived like birds, huddling from the rain. The Koreans and the earlier Vietnamese had long since moved away.

Two blocks on the other side of "The Avenue" were The Projects, one story white barracks of welfare housing, built around two vacant, high-rise public housing towers. Across an isthmus that began where the subway opened up, there was another good neighborhood and then another, all of them connected by family one way or another and their hatred and fear of the "moolies," or blacks and the lower class Asians. The neighborhoods looked after each other and watched their borders.

When Venudo's convoy arrived, the loading zone in front of

Rosie's store had a delivery truck in it. Venudo double parked against it. Rosie drove up on the sidewalk, which was a common practice on her block where parking was at a premium. Orange had pulled ahead and was waiting across the street.

Traffic backed up and there was a lot of honking and yelling. Couington came down the street and showed his shield. The cars backed out except for one driver who was high and didn't "give a good goddamn." When huge cop told him to "button it," the driver knew he meant it.

Mastrangelo's grocery store had been in her family for fifty years. It occupied 317 and 319 South Mildred Street, which were connected so that the store on the bottom would have a double front. The upstairs on the left had been rented out for years to Rosie's uncle, but he had died. Now it was used for storage by a furniture store down the street.

Officer Mastrangelo did a room to room search since she knew the place best. Venudo stayed downstairs in the front of the store with Maya. Johnson went around back and waited in the rear. There were cellar doors in the front and the back that went down in through the sidewalk, one for store deliveries and the old one for coal.

Eugene, "Hugey," who worked in the store, was paying for the delivery of bread, so Venudo knew that the truck parked in front was legitimate. When Rosie came back downstairs, they took Maya upstairs and checked next door on either side. The sector patrol car that Venudo had called arrived and parked in back in the playground at St. Theresa's. The whole thing had taken less than ten minutes.

After everybody settled in, Rosie started a pot of tomatoes, onions, and garlic. Her kitchen was small, but seemed longer because of the bay window that let light in from the front room. Maya sat at the table wanting to smoke.

"It isn't right," Venudo said, pouring a little wine in the sauce they called "gravy" and fishing out a bay leaf. "It's too, too...."

"Something," the other two cops said together, finishing the statement that he made each time he tasted anybody else's cooking.

"You want to help me in the kitchen?" Rosie asked. "Those men think only they can cook." Maya had moved to the small front parlor. She was reading the paper and watching television. "I garden better than I cook," she answered.

Rosie went downstairs to the store for two green peppers. When she left the kitchen, Al went out into the hall so he could see Maya. She had her feet up and was clicking through the stations and rubbing her forehead. There was a window in the parlor so he had Maya move her chair. "So the light won't be in your way," he told her.

Two Laotians were in the store. Hugey had just put provolone on the slicer, but walked back to the counter. He didn't like them. They were little and dirty, but he sold them their milk and bananas and the Marlboro's which they smoked, squatting on the sidewalk like they were taking a shit, he thought. He picked out two nice peppers and handed them to Rosie, who did a little juggling act with them as she went back upstairs.

Carlo Gigante, "Jimmy Two Plates," came in the store. The old man wore a felt fedora with the brim up all around and had on very thick glasses for his diabetes-ruined eyes. As always, he wore a suit jacket, although it didn't match his pants, and a starched white shirt. Some said his glasses made him look like his uncle, "Jimmy Bottles," who had died in Lewisburg Penitentiary in 1972.

He took two of the rolls that just came in for the provolone Hugey would slice for him. When he got back to the Columbus Social Club, Carlo would make "sangwitches" with romaine lettuce and real extra virgin olive oil, sprinkling on his own oregano and black pepper.

"This O.K., Mr. Gigante?" Hugey asked him, holding up a slice of the cheese. Hugey never called him "Jimmy" out of respect, although Jimmy Two Plates sometimes told him to.

Lately, Carlo sometimes remembered himself as Carlo Gigante and sometimes as "Jimmy Two Plates." More and more he thought of himself as "Chingy," which was what he was called at St. Monica's, the parish he moved from when he was twelve. Carlo leaned forward so he could see the slices of cheese. "That's nice," the old man answered. He picked out a tomato which he handed to Hugey.

Hugey weighed and wrapped Mr. Gigante's cheese and gave him two packs of Lucky's with the rolls and tomato. The old man took his package and left without paying. He paid a hundred dollars at a time and Rosie kept the tab.

Dr. Charcot went upstairs. The smell from the kitchen was rich, but she was not interested. There were two maple beds in the room and a matching desk and chair between them. On the night table was a lamp with a rose cut into the shade. It matched the wallpaper of little rosebuds that went out into the hall. Maya tried to sleep, but couldn't. She looked for an ashtray.

Officer Mastrangelo knocked on the half-open door, peering in so she could see that everything was all right. "You wanna beer?" she asked. "I got Coors Light."

Maya answered, "Not now, thanks."

Rosie told her to use the bathroom down the hall rather than the one next door which had the door closed. She told her that the toilet was broken because the bathroom was in a sight line from the open parking lot in the back.

"You could smoke if you want to," Rosie told her. "I used to, but I quit. I'll get you an ashtray."

"Thanks," Maya said. "I've got to quit too. You're being nice to me. Thank you."

"No problem," Rosie answered. She went down the hall thinking about the Newports she used to smoke.

Maya wrapped her feet up in the bottom of the blanket and started to doze, but Venudo called, "Dinner is served," and Maya didn't want to be rude. They ate in the kitchen. There was homemade wine. Maya had three glasses. Venudo had none.

After her second glass of wine Maya said, "I feel like Anastasia," which nobody got.

Al Couington asked, "Albert Anastasia?"

That made them all laugh except Maya. Rosie explained that

Albert Anastasia was a mob guy who "got clipped" in a barber shop. That got everybody laughing again including Maya, who said she felt like Lou Costello.

Venudo, corrected her, "Frank Costello, maybe, you mean?"

Dr. Charcot answered, "Who's on first?" laughing from the wine.

Maya helped Rosie with the dishes, then went back upstairs and watched TV until eleven. When she thought she had the place to herself, she called home to listen to her messages. There were two. One was from Swift and one was a wrong number. She had hoped to hear from Ashman even though he usually did not call. This was especially so when he had "something to do," which she knew meant he had an assignment, or "a place to go" he called it.

Maya took a long shower even though the door wouldn't lock. She tried to make herself comfortable in bed, creating a little nest for herself with the blanket and moving her feet back and forth which helped her fall asleep.

Twice that night she awoke, the first time thinking she was home, then that Ashman was there. Maya Charcot thought it was a time when she was on the back porch dusting her plants and he had come in from the shed. He was wearing white carpenter's pants with loops on the legs and a red silk vest with birds on it.

Ashman held two metal soldiers, the kind he collected. He had an Indian, one with a curved sword in one hand, and in the other hand, the kind of Indian with a bow and arrow. He smiled when he walked towards her.

Maya fell asleep and into another dream. In the dream, Maya went over to water the metal soldiers she had just been thinking about. She felt like water as she walked. The watering can was bright shining copper with a silver spout. She turned the soldiers over. Their bottoms were red, green and yellow ceramic put together like a puzzle. There were little embryos sprouting out. She tried to read the colored puzzle, but it changed as the sprouting grew.

When Maya woke up, the room was too warm and Rosie was mouth breathing in the other bed. Maya could see Rosie's shotgun against the wall side of her bed.

Venudo was down the hall. He had brought his Beretta 390. It didn't take a loading tube, but he wouldn't part with it. On the stock he had hand-lettered the New Testament quotation from Luke, "When a strong man fully armed, guards his own house, his possessions are safe." He stayed in the parlor and every hour through the night he checked the inside perimeter.

Maya did not feel safe. She felt dislocated and tangled and she wished she was home or that Ashman was there. She went down to the kitchen to drink some iced tea and smoke a cigarette.

Couington Johnson met her. He sat with her for a while. They didn't say much. He talked to Maya about cats when Rosie's big mouser came up to stare at the bottom of the stove. Maya poured herself another glass of wine which she took upstairs and said goodnight.

There were noises out front twice that night, but they were nothing. Couington heard something in the back around 2:30, but stayed at his post. If something went down, the sector car was there and he knew not to be pulled away from his spot. At 3:30, the uniformed sector cop pulled his blue and white over and knocked on the door so he could take a piss. He wanted to stay and chat, but Couington walked him to the door and told him he'd bring him a hot coffee.

Rosie Mastrangelo was straightening the kitchen when Maya came downstairs in the morning. "Did you sleep good?" she asked.

"Restless, I guess."

"This'll be over soon. Then you can go home. You want a piece of pie? I've got apple and rigot."

"Sorry?"

"Rigota, cheese pie. You'll love it. Me, I'm on a diet, but I'll join you to be sociable," Rosie answered, smiling.

They each had a slice of pie and coffee and sat around. Dr. Charcot smoked, but when she saw Rosie wanted one, she put it out. Then Maya went back upstairs and fell asleep.

She dreamt about the hotel explosion: the deafening noise, the way the lights flashed and the police looked and the way the dark waves of the lake had gone through the night. Maya felt awful when she awoke again, shaken and with the strong feeling that someone evil was in the room.

Commanche Moon

A shman went back to Maya's and waited for the enemy. No one came. In the morning, Major Coates called for him to come in at noon. Ashman got there a half hour early so he could walk around before going in for his appointment.

The Major came out himself and escorted Ashman into his windowless office. Rooms without windows disoriented Ashman like a black iron prison. He became distracted.

As Coates scrolled through his records on the computer, Ashman remembered how two years before in an office building that looked like a book standing on its edge, he had shot Attorney Beryl Green in the throat after removing a phony cast from his right arm. Green, the fat lawyer with the green tie and the emerald stick pin, died staring at the three arms on the desk across from him.

"Seems we were at the same place at the same time," Coates

said as he looked at the record of his dipper's wartime service.

Ashman thought he should say something, "I guess it's all the same, Major," he answered.

Major Coates nodded and gave Ashman his assignment. Both the Major and the Advanced Research Project Agency and he personally needed impenetrable insulation around them. For that, the Major needed Frankie Cigars dead.

Frankie had rendered services to Uncle Sam as far back as Nixon, but lately he was acting like a partner. When Dakkas and Frankie Cigars had last met on Frankie's boat off of Mantauk Island, Frankie told Dakkas, who he thought was FBI, that he needed his nephew to get a pass on a drug bust and that "he was due that, his work for Uncle Sam being an investment that was earning compound interest."

The Major thought of using Dakkas to take Frankie Cigars out, but that would have looked like an FBI double cross and that could mean the Mafia would no longer be available as a resource. The Major also thought he was overusing Dakkas.

"Sal Ciccione, 'Frankie Cigars,' does some work for us now and then," he told Ashman. "But he's not such a good idea anymore. His 'bizz-i-ness' is getting in the way. And," Coates paused, "there's preliminary information that he had something to do with the explosion at the New Conquistador Hotel."

Ashman's pulse quickened at bit, but his eyes did not flicker. He didn't like this.

"One of ours, Dakkas, said you were there. Lorraine Knoddles, I understand you knew her. That's too bad."

Ashman wondered what Dakkas was doing there and why

the Major had told him. Was he covering an attempted hit on Maya? Or was the explosion meant for both of them? "Dakkas?" he asked.

"He was on another assignment." the Major answered. "Make Frankie Cigar's death look like a family dispute, a mob thing."

It smelled bad to Ashman, but he knew that once Uncle Sam gave you a job, you couldn't say no because then you were part of it. Major Coates gave him all the information he needed for Frankie Cigars. The dossier included some intel on Ray Sabatino, Franca's live-in. Ashman half-smiled at that.

"By the way," the Major said as he got up to leave, "Sabatino's a little present for you. Word on the street is that he's been looking for you. And while you're here, you're due for your ten thousand mile check-up. You haven't been in for a while. We got a lot here," he said patting his terminal, "but your check-up, we need that every now and then. See my receptionist on the way out. I think you start at room 101."

Ashman knew the battery of tests would take him almost three hours. He thought it was largely bullshit, but he had no choice and hoped that he might find out something about what had put him in the hospital. When Ashman got to room 101, there was a note that the clerk was out to lunch. He waited for almost an hour reading magazines and remembering when he had first met Coates in Vietnam.

* * *

Ashman had come circling in through the kunai grass to the circumference of Fire Base Marie. He was ahead of Captain

Coates, who was coming back into his fire base with his thirty man platoon. Coates was trying to squeeze and fry 'the little man', who had been dropping their mortars on his camp. From the way Coates walked, Ashman thought he might have seen him before in Saigon.

Captain Coates had stripped the land around his base so that his perimeter was an open field. It was clear up to the kunai grass on one side and to the elephant grass on the other two and down a sloping hill to the road and the jungle that grew up to it.

There had been big trees in the rear of the camp with thick trunks, but the Captain had chopped them down along with the buffalo. Coates used the 700 yard range of his fifty caliber weapons and the withering fire of his two Vulcans to keep his back porch clean. The electronic gattling guns were mounted on armored personnel carriers and delivered thousands of rounds per minute, whirling and flashing.

Two young girls in baseball caps went halfway into the elephant grass to meet the thirty man platoon, sliding barefoot around the cutting blades of grass, twisting their feet to the outside as they walked to avoid the wounds the grass could make and the sores that would never heal. "My beah ice cold! My Coke number one! Her number ten o.d. piss," they called.

Captain Coates waved his men off and they had to settle for Kool Aid and cheap cigars. Ashman was waiting and saw the two Lurps come in from across the road and through the dirty stream. Nobody looked at them for more than a moment.

The Lurps stayed off towards the side. The shorter one, who Ashman took for Tubman, held up two fingers, "Cold ones!" he called. He wore a black bandanna over the top of his face with holes so his eyes could look through. He had a tiger paw around his neck, a souvenir from the eight foot magical beast they had killed to convince the Bru's to join the other Montangards as mercenaries, the Bru's who ate the filthy rats around the camp and from the tunnels as if they were roast chicken.

"Cold ones!" he said again. "Tell the butterbar we need six cold ones!" He swung his sixteen gauge from around his back. Ashman wondered whether the Lieutenant would respond.

The other Lurp was taking a piss against the hot shit cans, standing behind the oily smoke billowing out of the fifty gallon drums, pissing and watching the steam he made. That was likely Metaphor, which meant to Ashman that Smiley was still out there. Together they were called 'The Cambo Ghost,' and they worked both sides of the river.

Like all the Lurps, they had been out too long. They would have to stay out forever or either come in and short circuit somewhere quick, or be very dangerous until they got shut down. They were covered with jungle filth and killing filth.

The E-5, brought them a cold six pack. Metaphor took the ax from behind his back and cut the tops of the beers off toma-hawk-style. Ashman watched them drink and Metaphor clean the carbon off his AK-47 with the beer and the tooth brush that he wore around his neck. Ashman walked in slow, holding up a picture of Father Trabant, who was his assignment. "I'm here for him," Ashman said.

"Lai di," Metaphor called over his shoulder, smiling. "Come here." Nobody came. He wore a CVC on his head, but the communicator helmet had no hook-up and afforded no safety. His head was shaved clean with a blue line down the center. They started to laugh, Tubman and Metaphor, but only one of them outloud, Metaphor showing his teeth, every other one painted black.

"You got our DD214's?" Metaphor asked Ashman, still laughing and showing his painted teeth. "We're all waiting for our discharge papers. Got to get back to The World. Gotta hook-up to that Twenty-Four Hour Generator. We're all fadin' in and out."

"Chieu Hoi!" Tubman called out, "Give it up, Smiley. Come on back in."

"We're on S and D forever, brother," he told Ashman. "Search and Destroy from here to the end of time and then back again. Make sure nuthin's still breathin'. Don't you know who we are?" he went on. "We're the fuckin' Cambo Ghost. Been riding the River and straddling Route 9 like bitches in heat. Can't come in. It'll burn us. Our sit rep is fucked." He shook his head back and forth. "We can't come in. We're in another place and we can't come in until 2012. Sometime in December, I think. We're lucid and paranoid at the same time."

Ashman saw a sparkle off a barrel 200 yards out. "That must be Smiley showin' off," Tubman said. "Tell the Reluctant that he's cured himself. He don't need no hospital ship. He just cut it out, lopped it off. Anyways, that's as far as he'll come in. Says this is all of the World he can take. That it'll make him radioactive. Can't take no dangerous visions. He's living natural now. Naked as a jaybird. Painted himself all over, eatin' monkey and talkin' to them. Tied his dick down. He's a double veteran backwards several times, you know. He ices them, then he mounts them. That's not countin' bear, buffalo, and his monkey friends. Can shoot the pubic hair off a flea at a thousand yards."

Tubman came back from pissing on the cans again and began preparing some opium to smoke. Metaphor got up.

"Not him," Ashman said.

"Not who?" Metaphor asked.

"Not him, Smiley. Not him."

"Who?"

"My op," Ashman said, holding up the photo again.

"Your op, that's bad mojo. Father Trabant, he's taken to the catacombs. We lost him in the tunnels. Tubman here's the best tunnel runner there is, but the mojo man kind of just disappeared. There must be a false bottom or a whole other world somewhere. Anyways, he's sure gone 200 percent native as far as we can tell. Anyways, tell the FNG back there that we're the Blackhawks now. I'm him and my brother here is Andre or Olaf and Smiley's Chop-Chop."

The two Lurps picked up their gear and three cartons of Kools that the E-5 brought. They went back across the thin dirty stream and across the road. Then the Company scout, whose name was Daniels, came over to take Ashman out.

The scout had raised scars on his cheek and two clefts in his chin, one from his lineage and one from a fleshette mine. Daniels smelled the air around Ashman. He did not smell aftershave or soap, but there was no three week sweat or insecticide either. He thought maybe Ashman just rotated back in. "Don't touch nothing," the scout said. He went off at a run, neither he nor his gear making any sound.

They stopped only twice, once for a barrel flash off to the East and once for a boobytrap, two bamboo snakes hanging in tubes to the left of a trip wire. Ashman got to the coordinates exactly on time.

The tunnel rat lifted a grass flap which opened in front of Ashman, and came up whistling. "I'm Steamboat Willie," he said. "Us Bobcats, the 1-5, are the best tunnel men there is." He tilted back his hat. "You claustrophobic? Hate rats? Not to worry. The ones down here don't carry no plague. We're going downstairs now. Do what I do. Go where I go. Don't touch nothing. There's no rank down here. Never cross over. Never walk across no chamber. Stay behind me. Don't touch nothing. I'm always whistling 'Dixie' when I come up so we know it's me. If you gotta go up without me, you do the same. Or 'Over the Rainbow'."

Steamboat Willie held his light on a stick as they went down. The first part down was the most dangerous, where they'd hang you up, stab you in the nuts, he told Ashman. You could kill a man that way. He carried a .22 and a Bowie knife, and wore homemade knee pads. Ashman wore his .45, a boot knife, and a Tokorev .762 flat against his back. He had taken the automatic from a Red Chinese officer a month ago.

They traveled fast and then slow and fast again, like someone was following them, stopping when the running of the rats under the floor boards above them got too loud. Twice they went flat for the rats to run over them.

The tunnels went from hardly wide enough for them to get

through, to wide enough to drive a truck. The walls were hard and smooth like clay. They came to a wide turn to the right and a narrow one to the left. "Food depot," the tunnel rat whispered, pointing to the right. "No more rats for a while."

Steamboat took them down some steps and to the left again. When he held up a closed fist, they stopped. Then he flattened them out and they listened. It was quiet. Ashman could smell water. They went ahead and came upon a well. It was dug deep into the tunnel floor and the water smelled cold and dark. The tunnel rat backed up and spoke into Ashman's ear, "The hospital's up ahead."

The tunnel rat scouted the catacombs ahead. When he returned, they followed the left tunnel like a turning hallway. It took them to two large rooms filled with makeshift hospital equipment, parachute silk, and carpentry tools. There were empty boxes from black market U.S. drugs. The beds and chairs were empty.

"They've left it all behind," he told Ashman.

That was where Father Trabant was to be, where he came to meet with Dr. Quyen, who he had known since the French had let the Japanese in. The priest and the doctor shared Cuban cigars and hatred of the Colonials since then.

No one was there. Steamboat Willie turned around and they followed the tunnels back out. Someone else would be sent to cut the priest's throat.

He brought Ashman back out to the company scout, who took him back in. Ashman went back to La Bao and then flew out on a Caribou carrying radios and electrical parts. He debriefed in a pinkish light at the Two Swans Bar in Saigon across from the Hotel Parisian. Then he took some time in Tokyo.

When Ashman returned to Khe Sahn it had become a bloody dream, Westmoreland and the State Department, running back and forth, sometimes together, sometimes slow, sometimes dancing, sometimes bumping into one another. They dreamt that they were fighting the final great war against the Nazis while General Giap sent his race of little men down and around the futile fortress at Khe Sahn.

Soon the red clay at the Khe Sahn was mixed with black; oil black, carbon black, explosives black, burning black, no moon, no dreaming, no sleeping black, and then red again, leaking, seeping, shiny slippery red, pumping, squirting, spraying red, sometimes deep venous red, dark artery red, almost black, and then black again from the oil black and the burning black and always the screaming, screaming, screaming; the terror and the horror.

The only way out was to wait for the Commanche moon to light up the night. Then Ashman, who was both there and not, who saw, and smelled and heard and felt, but as someone else, could go out fast by the full light moon until the enemy stopped to rest or sleep and then, if he could, he killed them all.

* * *

When the clerk returned from lunch, he couldn't find Ashman on the schedule. Ashman was agitated from waiting, and said that if it wasn't straightened out fast "he wasn't the only one who would get an exam." It took a number of phone calls, but ten minutes later, the clerk said, "Through the door and down the hall. Dr. Idaho will see you."

Ashman went down the hall and turned to the left. It reminded him of the Elms for a moment, which made him a little dizzy. He took a deep breath and brought his mind back.

A technician named Beltz took blood pressure, height, and weight. Beltz was chewing gum to hide his cigarette breath. The tech sent Ashman across the hall to give his urine, "Cup's on the tank. First stream," Beltz said. He left for a smoke in the fire tower. "Leave it on the shelf," he called over his shoulder.

Ashman went next door where another technician, a pale blonde woman with a big nose, took his EKG. Ashman thought she must have been there a while, because his scars and the rot on his leg didn't seem to register on her. The test ran long because one of the suction cups kept coming off his leg.

Afterwards, they sent him to another room where he had to wait again. After another thirty minutes, a fat psychologist with a handle-bar mustache came in. Ashman disliked the testing, and the fat shrink.

"Dr. Idaho?" he asked.

"Excuse me?" asked the psychologist who was curling his moustache with his fat fingers.

"Idaho. Dr. Idaho. I'm supposed to see him."

"I'm taking her place today."

"Who?" Ashman asked again.

"Dr. Ho, not who. Ida Ho. I'm taking her place today. She's out sick," the psychologist said. "I'm going to give you some tests. They are called the MMPI, Graham-Kendall, and Cobby Reivich tests."

Ashman finished them as quickly as he could and went next door for his physical. He remembered the doctor had been a SEAL and was all right. The doc still had that lean and mean look, even though he smiled when he spoke.

"How do you do?" Dr. Rittenberg asked. "I don't like docs either."

Rittenberg did an orthopedic exam, pushing against Ashman's limbs and noting the restricted range of motion of his left wrist and of his neck. The right knee was a bit unstable on abduction. Next, he gave Ashman a neurological with a series of pin pricks and by checking his eyes and asking him to stick his tongue out.

He looked at the still visible I.V. tracks Ashman had gotten in the hospital. "We got a problem here?" he asked.

"I got a dose of dysentery. Was on I.V.'s for a week."

Dr. Rittenberg ran his fingers over Ashman's old scars and looked at his skin rot which covered his feet and up one shin. Then he slid across the floor on his chair and looked at Ashman's chart, "Let's see. You've taken Nizoral, topical and p.o., Fulvicin, and Mycostatin."

"Also some gray and green capsules," Ashman told him. "'Acoban,' I think."

"Ancoban," the doc noted, adding it to the chart.

"Right, and Loprox." I also tried soaking them in Clorox and in water some with some purple pills."

"Try some Lotrisone. You'll need a script. Otherwise, you're about the same as last time. Take care." He wrote out the prescription and slid back across the floor to shake hands.

Next, Ashman went to the pistol range. The elevator down smelled from the gun powder and lead which the shooters brought up with them.

"How the hell are you?" the rangemaster , whose name was Monty Gelman, asked. He wore half-glasses on his nose like a banker.

"You?" Ashman asked as they shook hands.

"I'm still scratching. I see you're still running."

"Through the concrete and under the dog shit. What's up with the bifocals?"

" I had to make sure I could see which direction to point these things," Monty said.

"I heard that. See any of the old guard around?"

"Same old same old. Some of the guys you know been around. Sammy Rynes, Misher, Colby," Gelman told him.

"Dakkas?" Ashman asked. The fact that he had been at the explosion or the Major said he was made him a potential enemy. "We were supposed to hook up. Shoot for beers."

"About a week ago," the rangemaster told him. "Shot pretty good. Anyways, you're ready for the usual. See if you can hit the side of Yankee Stadium without shooting your dick off. You haven't been around awhile. We got some new carnival rides." He gestured down the alley. "They got two cameras each. Part of your eval. You can watch it after."

Ashman left his belongings in the locker and picked up ears and glasses. Monty gave him a Smith and Wesson Model 640, a .357 with a shrouded hammer and a $2^{1/2}$ inch barrel and Model 4013 that stacked ten rounds, with one in the chamber. He walked Ashman out to the twelve point range and picked him a spot, taking the stapler out of his pants to put up the targets.

Hanging over the entrance to the range, was a sign that Gelman made. It was a quote from Jeff Cooper, "Don't handle dangerous game with little guns." The rangemaster always pointed to it as he walked his people to their shooting points.

The range was new and clean. The dozen points had holographic targets. The carnival rides were situation rooms where they played hijack, break-out and hostage.

When Ashman did anything for anybody else to see, he was a different person. Knowing he was on tape, he made his movements a little wider and slower and added a subtle hitch. When he was in the situation rooms, he changed his angles of position and dominance and his holding planes. Ashman shot from the Chapman-Weaver stance he usually used, but when he shot from behind the barricades, he crested the muzzle a bit high.

When he was done shooting, he leaned into the cage where the rangemaster was taking inventory. He wanted to see Dakkas' tape. "You gettin' lunch?" he asked.

"I bring it, but I'll have a Coke to leach the lead," the rangemaster answered. He came out and locked his cage. They went out and down the hall to the lunch room and talked about guns while they ate.

Monty Gelman thought laser sites were stupid, even Lasermax, "Who looks to see they got a red dot on them? They're okay for some training, except then you have to reompensate." He told Ashman that Mossberg had bought Savage Arms and that the Wesson company was in the toilet.

Ashman reminded the rangemaster how the two of them and the other Colby once spent an afternoon shooting-up out of date ammo with two AR-18's and a H & K, 5A3. They figured they shot up about ten thousand rounds. "Shoot 'till you puke," they had called it.

"Good times," Monty said as he finished his cold meatloaf sandwich.

That and some more of the "good old days" was enough for Ashman to see Dakkas' tape. Maybe Dakkas made alterations, too Ashman thought, but his general configurations would be the same and maybe Dakkas was too full of himself to hold back much. In either case, Ashman figured he could tell what was real and what was not.

He washed up well and left to complete the assignment that Major Coates had given him.

Kill Shot

A shman drove through the night with his sniper's rifle in his trunk and a Glock .40 within his reach. A second handgun was in the back seat for his escape route; over the seat, out the passenger's side back door, and behind the car.

He knew that New Jersey did not tolerate unlicensed firearms, even for cops from over the bridge. New York was just as bad. However, he was on the job for Uncle Sam, so he had "Do Not Detain" status. More importantly, when he was in the field, Ashman did not hesitate to bring his tools, no matter where he was.

Ashman had thought of flying to the Frankie Cigars job. He could have made appropriate arrangements for his weapons, even the one in the trunk, but he liked driving at night when he could examine the diagram that was forming in his mind.

His thoughts came together like the lines on the walls and

ceiling of the Chesapeake Bay Tunnel. He thought about the scene, the atmosphere, his approach and exit. Any substantial risks would come afterwards if his intel was good. The actual shot was the easiest part. Frankie Cigars would be gone quickly.

The next rest stop on the turnpike was the same place he had hitched a ride with the First Cavalry trucker. The air was warm and dirty. Inside the rest stop there were three fast food places that came together like a triangle, but they were closed.

There were vending machines and a coin changing machine down the hall. Ashman stopped at the men's room on the way. The man at the urinal next to him was smoking a Lucky Strike from the licorice smell of it. The bathroom smelled like new disinfectant and old piss.

Ashman got a candy bar and a soda from the vending machine and drove north. The highway was chopped-up and the lanes narrowed because of repairs. There were flashing arrows and bright lights. Ashman looked for the workmen, but there weren't any. He put his right hand on his Glock as he drove through the construction area, but nothing happened.

Ashman thought about the First Cavalry as he went ahead. He heard the "First Cav" song in his head: "First team, First Cav, black and yellow patch...." He put on a country western station to end it at that. Jack Kroner was singing about his old aching knees and his new jumping horse.

The Lucky Strike smoke in the men's room reminded him of a smell from somewhere else. First, Ashman thought he was remembering the smell of pot, or maybe of Camels or Kools in a jungle tent in the rain or something burning on the stove.

Then he realized it reminded him of something more chemical. He wasn't sure what.

Ashman drove out of New Jersey on his way to Buffalo, eating the candy bar and drinking his soda. As he was stopping to pay another toll, Ashman realized the smell was the cigarette smoke in the taxi the last thing before he woke up paralyzed in the hospital.

The drowning feeling came back for a moment and it choked Ashman. He remembered a long time ago finding a corpse hung-up in a flooded viaduct. The face was swollen and the color of rotten fruit. The arms and legs were waving in the current. Then he thought about the two madmen from the Elms, their heads bobbing up and down, and the one running around with his arms flapping, and the weird storyteller, who smelled like cooked onions and who had pulled the catheter out and saved him.

Ashman focused his attention on what happen to him in the taxi. He could see the cabbie's face blowing the smoke out. That didn't make sense because he remembered sitting in the back of the cab. He could see how light the cabbie's eyebrows were, as if he didn't have any at all, and that his hair was thin and wispy. Again Ashman saw the driver blowing the smoke over the back seat at him.

He realized at that moment how he had been taken-out. It was that cigarette smoke in the cab. Probably scopolamine, an old European tactic often used to shanghai tourists. For a moment he smiled.

Now he knew he would get them back. Ashman felt like he had grabbed them by the end of a rope which he'd hand over hand until he got them. He would cut their throats when he did, and while they choked on their blood, he'd stuff their dicks in the bloody slits. He had done that before, to serve his Country, doing "black ops" across the border into Cambodia. Now he would do it for himself.

Ashman went over that taxi ride in his head; the route, the way the cab looked inside and out. The only other person at the cab stand at the train station that night was a tall black woman with light hair and a long green coat. The cab was a green and white Victory cab. He couldn't remember the number or any other intel on the driver. The taxi driver was his main quarry. That was where the trail of his memory took him and he trusted that.

Realizing that he was thinking past the job at hand, he slowed himself down and went over his Frankie Cigars plan again, step by step. Ashman looked at the contingencies and visualized how everything would go from that moment on like a familiar path appearing as he went along.

The actual shot was one that he had made a dozen times. He would take it in a sitting position because of the angle of the cover. Ashman saw it unfold, and how it would look through the Leupold scope. He felt the recoil. The .308 Winchester Supreme was a store-bought bullet which gave the job the anonymity he wanted, but the notched hollow points made them one shot stops. His weapon, the Robar QRZ-F mini sniper rifle, weighed only eight pounds. The job would be clean and quick.

That out of his mind, he drove on to get Ray Sabatino. The Major had warned him. And if Sabatino hadn't sent someone after him already, he would be doing that soon.

It was just getting light when Ashman arrived in Buffalo, so he drove to Doyle's. The place was closed and there was a "For Sale" sign on the house next door. He shook his head when he thought of Eggs Doyle dead and clenched his hands on the steering wheel. He wondered about Doyle's wife. Doyle said she was as good an old lady as there was.

There was a diner up the street where they had eaten lunch a couple of times. The place looked different to Ashman as he drove up and he wondered whether the parking lot in front had been widened.

"Joe," he told the girl behind the counter.

She looked at him. "Who?"

Ashman looked at her.

"Joe?" she asked.

"Coffee, black," he told her.

"I got ya, hon. We got a special today, two eggs, sausage patties, home fries, coffee." She had pasty white skin.

"S.O.S.," added the owner, who was filling ketchup bottles.

"Chipped beef on toast, coffee," she translated.

"That comes with juice," the owner said.

"Orange, pineapple, grapefruit, out of tomato," the waitress told Ashman. "Get the large, the small's a shot glass."

She took his order and went to wait on the two men who sat near the window. Ashman saw that one of them carried a valise. The other, who was left-handed, was wiping the table down with a napkin.

"I'm a friend of Doyle's," Ashman told the owner who had walked up.

"Mickey Doyle?".

"No. Down the street. The tappy."

The owner looked at him.

"The taproom, the saloon, Eggs Doyle."

The owner realized Ashman was talking about the killings down the street. "Niggah bastads," he said. His hatred and his Boston accent came out when he got angry. "I'll help lynch them rotten bastads," he went on.

"They make a pinch yet?" Ashman asked him, adding, "an arrest" so he wouldn't have to translate further.

"Not yet. Them savages still on the loose."

"He was a friend of mine," Ashman said. "His missus okay?"

"She died right after them animals got him and what's his name, the big guy, the doorman."

"Finnegan," Ashman told him. "He was Doyle's nephew."

"It's vile, fucking vile."

The waitress brought him a second orange juice. "Homemade barbecue comin up for lunch," she said. "I made it myself," the owner added.

Ashman drove back to Doyle's and parked across the street. He thought he saw the neon sign flashing, but it was reflected light. The two men who had breakfast at the diner drove by.

He followed them for a mile and a half before they pulled into the hospital parking lot and a "Physicians Only" space. He waited until they went in and after fifteen more minutes went for Ray Sabatino. Ashman wanted revenge now, not just pre-emption. It was on him like an angry shadow.

He drove to Franca's and parked at the bottom of the field behind her house to recon the property. If Sabatino wasn't there, he'd go to his restaurant and then his house.

Ashman came across the macadam road and up across the field, moving low and fast. There was a new glider out back and a cat sleeping on it. It was the cat he had seen before. A Maxima, like Franca's, was in the driveway. There was a straw handbag on the back seat of the car and a dolphin mobile hanging from the mirror.

He swept around the house and looked in the windows. Sabatino wasn't there. Franca came out for the paper. The big orange and white cat came around to meet her. Ashman left.

As he drove to Sabatino's restaurant, Ashman calmed himself and focused on the next alternative in his plan. The restaurant was closed. A new Chevy was in the back. A light was on in the kitchen. He went up the three steps and looked in the window. Ray Sabatino was banging a redhead against the counter. She had her legs around him and was steadying herself with her hands.

"Make it a quickie, Big Ray," Ashman said. He wanted to kill Sabatino right there, his dick out and his pants around his ankles, but that would mean killing the woman too, and he didn't know enough about her to do that safely.

A bakery truck pulled up. The girl heard it and apparently so did Ray, because he picked up the pace. She was banging her head on the over-head light fixture. When they finished, the redhead went to clean up and drove Ray three blocks where she let him out at a gas station.

They didn't kiss good-bye and the woman didn't wait for him. While Sabatino was paying for his car, Ashman used the john at the gas station across the street. When Ray Sabatino drove away, Ashman followed him, staying two cars behind. He recognized the route. The prick was going to Franca's.

Sabatino stopped at a bakery. He came out with a tied white box and bag. At least the guy is nice enough to bring her some cookies. Maybe he even washed off his dick, Ashman told himself. He rolled down the window so he could take his quarry there, popping him through the white cake box he carried. Ashman imagined the blood running onto the little coffee cakes or the strawberry shortcake Franca liked so much, but a patrol car pulled up to the bakery. They drove ahead to Franca's.

After Sabatino had parked in her driveway, Ashman put Doyle's .45 in the wheel well of his trunk. He also put a phony ledger sheet and a detailed drawing of Doyle's bar in the glove box. Then he popped the hood and fouled the distributor. The whole thing took him under two minutes.

They were having coffee in her kitchen when Ashman left. Sabatino was pointing at Franca while he spoke and his face was getting red. Franca was giving it back to him.

Ashman drove out on to the interstate and called the police from a pay phone. "Detective McNamee?" he asked.

"Seventeenth precinct. The purpose of your call, please?" the intake officer asked.

"I'm calling from the Philly P.D. Friend of Johnny Reegan's." He remembered not to say "Raygan."

The other end was silent, so Ashman added, "Johnny Applesauce," but they had already put him on hold. McNamee answered. "What's up?" he said.

"I'm calling from the Philly P.D.. Friend of Johnny Reegan's, Applesauce. Calling about the Doyle case. Name's Chioveno," He started to spell it.

"So?"

"You wanna close this case?"

"What 'Doyle' case is that?"

"Don't shit me," Ashman told him. "If you want it, fine. If not, I'll give it to the State, to O.C.."

McNamee didn't want to give up the case particularly to the state's Organized Crime Bureau. OCB would rub his nose in it.

"Yeah, sorry. I'm being a dick," he said.

"It's the job," Ashman told him.

"Yeah, excess cash and time on my hands. What's up?"

"Ray Sabatino did the barroom hit. Doyle was late on his payments. I'm told he got Doyle's piece in his car, a Caddy. '99, gold. He'll be at 7012 Hilltop Road for a half hour. There's a woman in the house. She's not in this."

"Friend of yours?"

"Her dad was a friend of mine. She's a widow," Ashman answered.

"Maybe she needs a replacement. We'll pick him up."

When he heard the boredom in McNamee's voice, Ashman added, "Somebody else'll get him if you drag your ass."

McNamee didn't want someone else to clear the case. "I'm going off in ten minutes, but I'll take it. I never liked that prick."

"He's belligerent, McNamee. And he says you're all stupid."

"I hear ya," said McNamee. He got his partner and they went out to get Sabatino. They would have the sector car meet them. McNamee hoped it wasn't the new woman on patrol, who he knew would be no good as back-up. His partner hoped it would be, because she had great knockers.

Ashman would have liked to watch them pick up Sabatino, but his Frankie Cigars schedule was paramount. If they didn't collar Sabatino, or if Ray walked, he would kill him as he had originally planned.

The directions to Frankie's marina at Montauk were good. Ashman could see the marina from Route 209, but as he followed the exit ramp off, it disappeared behind the horizon and the black cars that drove by. When he got on to the service road, the marina appeared again. The water was blue with white boats. The water turned green and then dark blue, almost black.

He parked his car in the round shopping center across the highway and walked back to the service road with his collapsible sniper's rifle under his raincoat. There were parallel concrete drainage ditches along the service road and two open drains. He quickly crossed them and the field of high weeds and cattails that ran to the bridge abutment. To the east was a railroad yard at about 1000 yards, but it was deserted. To the south were more high weeds. There was more highway to the north. The sun was high and behind him.

Ashman climbed the embankment. As he crested it, he could see the marina again to the west. The water shone bright, but there was no glare. He wedged himself behind the concrete support of the bridge and looked through his scope for Frankie Cigars.

The cabin cruiser was in the third slip as it was supposed to be. Frankie Cigars was aft on his portable phone. There were three men on the bridge, drinking. One looked like Dakkas. Ashman didn't like that. He thought about taking him too, or packing up, but Ashman reminded himself that now was not the time to deviate.

He locked himself in place, sighted Frankie Cigars in, and exhaled. The shot was clean. Ashman saw Frankie's skull break off and fly away like a frisbee.

Dakkas took cover, waiting for another shot. Ashman packed up and drove back home wondering what was going on. The Major had put them together twice now, including at the New Conquistador Hotel.

He drove all the way back without stopping and went to his basecamp apartment. The room was small with one window and a bathroom off to the left. There was a sofa bed and a maple desk which he never used.

Ashman checked his messages, showered, and went to the train station to see if he could find out something about the green and white cab or the woman in the green coat. That night he slept a deep sleep.

Dakkas

No one was there when Emil Dakkas came home from the marina. His Great Dane was asleep down the hall and stood up when he opened the front door. The huge dog was formidable even from a distance and when he ran the length of the house for Dakkas to let him out, the china closet in the hall shook.

Dakkas had disengaged the magazine disconnect of his gun as he always did when he came in the house. When he went back out again to walk the dog, he squeezed the clip back in. They walked around the yard and when the dog was done marking his spots, Dakkas fed him. He knew that keeping the dog lean would extend the dog's life from seven or eight years to past ten. Even so, at one hundred sixty pounds, the Dane was only twenty pounds lighter than he was.

Dakkas could still smell the death of Frankie Cigars and the puke. He took off his clothes, showered, and wiped his shoes.

There were tiny stains on his clothes that might not come out.

He had spent the ride back from Montauk thinking about the shooting. He stood in the warm shower, thinking about it again, that a kill had occurred with him not twenty feet away. Was he the target or a secondary one? If the shooter had wanted him, there would have been time to take him out. Who was the shooter? Who sent him? Dakkas asked himself.

He covered his gun with his tee shirt as he dried off. Afterwards, he hung the wet towel over the bathroom door to dry and so his daughter couldn't accidentally lock herself in the bathroom. He put on his soft clothes, sweat pants, boat shoes, and a pullover and went downstairs.

There was a catalogue for bathroom fixtures open on the kitchen table and Emil looked at it as he ate a turkey sandwich. His wife, drove up. She had their daughter, Sonny, with her. Sonny was as light as they were dark. Emil noticed another little girl in the car. It was probably the Karentys' daughter.

Sophie pulled into the driveway, waving to Emil, who came out to meet her. The dog came out with him and was running around the car and jumping up. "Get down, get down," Sophie said. "You're scratching the paint."

When Dakkas spoke, the dog stopped.

"I'm back from dancing, Daddy," Sonny said as she ran up to Emil.

He picked her up and kissed her on the forehead. The dog came over and tried to wedge his way between them.

"Did you bring me anything?" she asked.

"Now, now," Sophie said.

"I did," said Emil. He gave her and her friend a stick of gum. The Dane sat, waiting for one. "One for you and one for your friend," Emil said. He gave her a second piece and whispered, "One more for good luck."

"Karla's going to stay for dinner," Sophie told him.

The dog came up to the girls, sniffing for a treat. Sonny gave him her stick of gum which he went away to eat.

When they were inside and the two girls were in front of the television, Sophie asked, "You all right?"

"Tough day," he told her.

"I'm sorry," Sophie said, putting her hand on his. "Remember, I've class tonight. I'll drop Karla off on the way. Can you give Sonny her bath?"

Emil had never gotten used to seeing his little girl naked, but he answered, "Sure I can."

"You want some tea? You okay?" she asked.

"I'm fine," he told her.

Sophie made Celestial Waves, which to Dakkas tasted like half of the herbal teas she bought. The other half tasted like mint. He cleaned up from making his sandwich as she made the tea.

"How's school?" he asked.

"Two more weeks, but my professor is a b-i-t-c-h."

"I know what that spells," Karla said from the TV room.

"Me too," said Sonny.

"Me three," said Emil.

"Oops," Sophie told them. "Sorry. Anyway, she looks like she hasn't slept in days. Like she's been living out of a suitcase. I've got all my outlines done. Getting ready for cram time."

"You studying with Sylvia again?"

Sylvia was her sister, dark like Sophie and Emil. Billy Orr, Sylvia's husband, was like Sonny, as light as they were dark. Sophie had made a joke about that once, about him and Sonny both being so light and Emil and her being so dark. Orr became agitated and went on and on how he'd never betray Emil. They didn't talk about that again.

"Starting Thursday. No, tomorrow night," Sophie answered, "She's coming over to study with me. Bill coming over?"

"He didn't tell me. I haven't seen him in a couple of days."

"How's he doing?" she asked him.

"Fine," he answered as he went outside for a smoke. The big dog followed him and lay on a pile of leaves with his front legs crossed in an "x." Dakkas walked and smoked and thought about how he came to be driving home with Frankie Cigars' brains on his clothes.

* * *

The next morning, Billy Orr was debriefed by Major Coates. Neither of them was happy about the shot Orr had missed.

The Major had directed Orr to take out the Mafia sniper,

who, unknown to Orr, was not a Mafia sniper at all, but Ashman, who had just killed Frankie Cigars. Major Coates was annoyed that the ASP, anti-sniper system had malfunctioned. He was more angry and concerned that his own system had failed. He wondered whether Ashman was the cause.

It was the second time that Ashman had escaped. The first time was from the Elms Hospital where the Major had stashed him so he would not interfere with the subversion of Maya Charcot's sound to light project. Coates was not concerned that Ashman would seek revenge for being shanghaied. Frankie Cigars had handled the details and Frankie was now dead. The Major wondered whether Ashman was "a disruptive factor" and wrote that on his yellow pad.

As Billy Orr went on with his description of what had occurred with the ASP, the Major became more agitated. It was almost as if there was another set of plans, another set of occurrences happening on its own. Major Coates could not see it all or where it was coming from. He knew that had to be resolved.

"I think I got feedback on my own light. Laser-rebound," Orr said, "I want to go downstairs to take a look before I write my report, if that's acceptable. Maybe the rangemaster has an idea."

The Major nodded, and Billy went down to the range. He went over the ASP apparatus with Gelman, who agreed it was laser rebound, but couldn't tell him exactly what the cause was. It could have been calibration, a manufacturing flaw in this particular weapon, or something in the system itself. Orr decided to include all of those possibilities in his report, which the Major would have on his desk the next morning.

Billy needed some release for his worry and anger. He went upstairs to the gym and worked the heavy bag, kicking it low and working his hands high. He switched stances and worked in quick, hard circles. The alarm on his watch went off. Orr quickly washed and left to pick up his wife.

Hunting

While Orr was debriefing with Major Coates, Ashman was hunting. He hailed a green and white cab and got in mumbling, so the cabbie, who had skin the coor of cedar, had to turn around to hear him through the yellowed plexiglass.

"Where?" the driver asked in a thick accent.

Ashman's eyes focused and refocused, seeing the cigarette in his mind. Because he wanted the driver long enough to get him talking, he directed him towards the suburbs. "Out to 69th Street," Ashman said. "I'll tell you from there, but I want to drive by the zoo first."

The cabbie had his two-way radio on, listening to crosstalk about jobs coming in. While he drove, he ate from a lunch box on the seat next to him.

"Business good? The Convention Center doing anything?" Ashman asked him.

"Slow, slow," the driver answered. He quickly changed lanes to avoid the gray van that cut him off. "Bastards!" he cursed, "Only the rich can get rich," he went on, rolling his "r's."

"I was surprised at the flat rate from the airport last week," Ashman told him. "When are they going to do that to you at the train station?"

"They do, I quit. Maybe I should go home. There, I drove a tank. It was safer there. Here, I have three jobs and I have to look out for the robbers and thieves and then they tell me 'straight fare.' No way," he said as he poured himself tea from his thermos.

Ashman went on, "I heard the same thing the other week from another one of you guys. I didn't get his name. White guy, light hair, like he had no eyebrows."

"I don't know. I don't know him. There are so many new drivers. They come and go. Me, this my seventh year. This is my cousin's cab."

Ashman needed more intelligence, but he knew he would get no more here. "I want to stop at the zoo," he said. He wanted to see the polar bears that rolled on the ice, and the butcher bird that impaled its prey and then ate it like an appetizer.

"No waiting. I don't wait," said the cabbie, putting his thermos back in his lunchbox. He pulled up to the entrance of the zoo. "I forgot to set the meter. Four dollars."

Ashman put his hand on the butt of his gun when the driver started to turn around. "Four dollars," the driver repeated. Ashman paid the fare and went into the zoo. Two men in gray uniforms were polishing the fountain of leaping antelope. Another crew was adding fiberglass to the home of the mountain sheep so they could look out across the skyline.

It had been dry and the zoo grass was brown. A car alarm went off in the parking lot which made the monkeys run up and down. A tiger roared and then another and all the flamingos rushed away.

Ashman went over and watched the polar bears. Two girls were standing in the cover of the arched brown wall that led to the thick window into the Arctic sea. One was trying to light a cigarette while the other offered her a shield against the breeze. She was wearing an army jacket with a peace sign on the back. Ashman thought she was Patty Valentine, Frankie's niece.

"It says 'No Smoking'," he told her.

"Eat me," the smoking girl said.

"Aren't you Patti Valentine? Frankie's niece?" Ashman asked.

"Who?" she answered with a sneer.

"Eat me twice," the other one said.

"It disturbs the bears and disturbs me," Ashman said, walking towards them.

"Whatever," the smoking girl said. She grabbed her friend by the arm. They walked away, stopping to give Ashman the finger.

He watched the two polar bears in the pretend sea for twenty minutes. The bird house was closed. Ashman leaned against a tree and watched the duck pond before he left. He looked for a cab back to the train station. There weren't any, so he walked.

Philadelphia has a big park system and some of the woods, not ten minutes away from the business district, were deep enough to get lost in. Maya and Ashman used to walk in Valley Green Park as the sun came up and they couldn't see the sky through the trees. She had a special down vest with military pockets that she wore whenever they went for walks. Ashman thought that was silly, but didn't say anything.

He liked the woods best when he went alone. The possibility of packs of wild dogs or men gave him his edge. The woods were thin over the two river drives, but the view was wide. He could see up the river to where it turned left out of his view. There was a highway and two bridges over it. The bridge abutments had become homes for bums.

Ashman went through the park towards town. He came out and across the overpass to the train station looking for a Victory cab, but there was none. There were two black women in long coats, but neither of them was who he was looking for.

He walked down to the University of Pennsylvania Hospital on Spruce Street. There were two green and white Victory cabs at the stand. One pulled away. It was driven by an Arab type, not Iranian like the tank driver, and carried a fat woman with a baby.

Ashman took the next taxi after waiting for the driver who had gone across the street to get a pair of hot dogs from the soda cart. The driver came back, walking so splay-footed that he looked like a clown. Ashman knew better than to discount him because of his appearance and that he could be the enemy.

"Where to?" Splayfoot asked, licking the mustard off his fingers.

"Delaware County Hospital," Ashman told him. He did not want two similar entries to be logged in. He could walk a mile to the bus and then catch something back out to Maya's. "Going to see my daughter-in-law. She got one kidney that don't work, so her husband, my wife's kid, drops her off and I wait for her dialysis. I take her home before her kid gets home from school."

"That's good," the cabbie answered. "That's a good thing."

"She's already there," Ashman said. "I get there about 2:30. She's done about five after three."

As he pulled away from the curb, Splayfoot popped open the soda can he had been holding between his legs. He took a long draught of the cold grape soda and belched. "Excuse me. I love grape soda, you know. Love it. I don't mean like it, I mean love it. I love it in the top five things of my life. I have three of 'em a day, every day. You want me to wait up there at the hospital?"

"That would be good. How much?" Ashman asked.

"I'll wait off the clock. Least I could do, tomorrow being Thanksgiving."

"You sure?"

"Yeah, sure. I get the fare back to your daughter's and I like a little snooze after I eat."

"I appreciate it." Ashman told him. "I use Victory all the time. I know some guys don't like to wait. This camel jockey, tank driver, wouldn't wait at all for me last week, on or off the clock. And the week before, this guy tells me he'll wait, but when I come back out, me and Marie, she's my daughter-in-law, we're standing in the rain, he's gone. What a prick!"

"What a prick is right," Splayfoot answered.

"I should make a complaint to his boss or the taxi commission or something. Light looking guy, wispy hair, real light eyebrows. I didn't get his name. Who thought I'd have to?" Ashman said.

"Don't know him. Must have been a temp. We get a lot of gypsy nomad types and college students."

"Nah, he was too old for that, the prick." Ashman ate a life-saver and offered one to the driver, but he waved it off.

"Got gum in my mouth. Grape gum," he said. "Sounds like a prick to me. You get his number?"

"License plate?"

Splayfoot pointed to the license on his visor, "No, I mean this."

"Nope. Guess I should forget it."

They pulled up to the hospital entrance. The building was old colonial with a new brick addition. It looked to Ashman like the one he saw in Buffalo when he followed the two doctors from the diner near Doyle's.

"I'll be out in twenty minutes," Ashman said. "If I'm longer, I'll come out and tell you."

"Okey, dokey," Splayfoot told him. "It's nap time." He

moved his chewing gum to his cheek and slid the front seat back. "It's nap time."

Ashman went inside and left by the side exit. He took the bus back to 69th Street. School was getting out, and seven junior high boys in their band uniforms got on at the next stop. He picked up part of a newspaper and sat behind it until they arrived at the terminal.

Ashman waited until everyone left the bus before he got off and walked over to the hot dog stand. He'd been wanting a hotdog with mustard since Splayfoot picked him up. He ate two and had a coffee. Then he found a pay phone. The booth stank, but he kept the door closed while calling to check on Maya.

Rosie answered. She was on her way to work, setting up for the Thanksgiving parade. It was a shitty detail and she wasn't happy.

"Steve there?" Ashman asked.

"Who's this?" she answered.

"Hal Jordan from the Two-Five," Ashman answered.

"Hey, Hal. He'll be right with you," Rosie answered, not recognizing his voice.

Hal Jordan was the Green Lantern comic book character and Venudo, who was a comic book freak, smiled when Rosie told him who was on the phone. "In brightest day in blackest night, no evil shall escape his sight," he told Ashman.

"Everything quiet?" Ashman asked him.

"Nice and quiet. You?"

"I gotta check on something."

"I gotta start the turkey. Come by. We'll all have dinner together. Just a few of us, me, the guys, you know."

"You want me to bring anything?" Ashman asked.

"Some red wine," Venudo told him.

"Bardolino?"

"Not too expensive, but no shit, please. And some parsley."

"No problem," Ashman said.

"We'll eat at my place. Rosie's pulled the f-ing parade." He pronounced it "prade." "She's none too pleased."

"Is Uncle Mike okay?"

"Yeah, he's fine," Venudo said, knowing Ashman was talking about Maya. "He's taking a siesta."

"Just tell him I called," Ashman answered.

"That's you, 'Hal Jordan: a man born without fear,'" Steve said.

"Yeah, see ya."

Ashman went to his car and drove to Maya's house to check on it. This time he went the fast way. As he came to the top of the hill around the bend to her house, he saw an electric truck pull away from the curb and go down the hill. Ashman went to the crest and saw it pull up to two men working down the street from Maya's. One of the men was going underground while one was standing outside the temporary yellow barricade they had erected around the open manhole.

Ashman didn't like the way things looked. He backtracked, parked his car two blocks away, and walked in, stopping behind a large tree to watch the two workmen.

"We'll pretend it's four o'clock," one said. "Then we can go home."

"Fine with me," said the other as he started to pack up.

Ashman went back to his car and followed it when they left. He stopped at his apartment to check his messages and his mail. Then he took a shower and went back in.

Running

Ashman's train ride into the city was slow and hot and when the train stopped, it was still in the tunnel. He walked quickly forward from the last car, leaving behind the other two passengers, an art student carrying a huge portfolio, and an old man with a broken arm. The subway concourse was up ahead to the left and a tunnel opened up to the sky to the right. Ashman could smell the rain coming down outside, bringing a memory that washed over him.

He had been underground in the tunnels in Vietnam with no rope around his ankle to pull him out. He had been in the trees in free strike zones, and in the jungle rain and the cold rain for forty days, so much rain that his clothes had become his skin and his skin had gone to rot that would last for thirty years. In his memory in the train station he was there again, in the tunnel, in the rain, in the memory that washed over him.

Ashman saw an endless sea of underground enemy in the

vast subterranean Vietnam space that the tunnel led to. It was an inside-out space, hollowed out for vast factories, hospitals, whole cities living under the surface of the earth. There were ladders with false tops, kitchens, aid stations, conference rooms, sleeping rooms and bomb shelters with conical roofs. Ashman had been sent into the tunnels and the underground living space to kill the Viet Cong's "Bob Hope", who did subterranean vaudeville shows.

It was not an underground sea of little men in black pajamas and costume shoes made from tire treads that he saw that last time in Vietnam and now again in his memory. It was an underground sea of moving ordinance and well-fed men with metal helmets and tanks, T-54's, and formations that arranged and rearranged.

At that moment, even when the First Infantry was strong and brave at Lai Khe, the 'Catcher's Mitt' they called that piece of ground, Ashman knew that the war was lost. The war was lost even if an eternal arc light came, the whistling death of ten thousand B52's. It was lost even if those planes dropped a million parcel bombs with their bouncing exploding, orange-looking killing things. It was lost even if a thousand, thousand spookys came for a thousand, thousand nights, and shone a million klieg lights and ate the earth with a million, million rounds.

He knew then, that at the heart of it, in the trees and underground, in the clay mud, black and red, in the hills and in French Saigon, that had become a Hollywood movie lot, what they had all denied as far back as An Khe and Route 19. The war was lost. All the reasons for the killing from then on were a lie.

Ashman had come up from the tunnels running to Loc Ninh to tell them of the formations and the tanks. He had run as fast as he could, running, falling, sliding. His legs were numb. His throat felt like broken razor blades and cold diarrhea ran down his leg. "The sit rep is fucked," Ashman told them. Then he went to dry his feet and drink hot, green tea. He sat off to the side, watching the men come in tiger stripes and profile suits. "Find, fix, and finish has it up the ass," he said, to no one in particular.

There were groups coming into Loc Ninh and going out. They were carrying strobe lights. Tubman was there again. He was wearing tuxedo pants and monkey hands, talking to a yard scout named Roy near a stack of radios that they had wired-up and hoped that the enemy would steal.

Metaphor, who was wearing a communications helmet and was painted black and white, was chopping off the tops of beers. He looked at Ashman quick and raised his ax, calling out a jungle call and smiling with his black and white teeth. Tubman came back, carrying some morphine and rounds for his AK. Ashman could see he wore all three tiger's paws around his neck.

The Lurps drank their beers, two each, and poured one on the ground. Then they went back out in their matching high top tennis shoes.

Now, Ashman began to run down the subway concourse, passing the people living in cardboard cities, derelicts and loons, and the stronger ones who preyed on them. "Spare change, spare change," said a woman in three coats, dragging a piece of striped awning. "Spare change, spare change," she said. She chanted as she walked, not to Ashman, not to anyone, looking for something metal to put on her head.

He ran by newsstands selling underground mints, a juice stand, shoe repairs and a candy store that did not see the light of day. There were three nurses holding hands, briefcase men walking by, school kids, a running dog, two transit cops, the big one chasing two young killers in black wool hats, and a blind accordion man playing "Silent Night," and selling white carnations.

There were rolling machines on the street above and he could hear them: cars, taxis, fire trucks with ladders, ambulances. There were plywood floats on Chevy frames that tomorrow would carry local weathermen, the shoemaker and the elves, and two real goats. The parade floats would be flanked by forgotten veterans in funny hats, waving politicians from the wards with too many toupees to mention, and girls with long, cold legs.

Ashman ran on in the subway tunnel and then up and out to Sansom Street which, like the street where he grew up, had a hardware store and laundromat. He had played on the stairs above that laundromat years ago, smelling the wet wash and the soap powder which made him sneeze. The nice old man, across the street, who had hair like Ginger Rogers and fat red hands, told stories to him in the laundromat and gave him caramels.

Above ground, Ashman ran past the crowds and cars until he was away and his mind cleared. He walked over to the liquor store for the bottle of Bardalino and a pint of Calvert. Bad white boys leaned against an old mail truck across the street. "How about a taste? Spare change?" they called to him as he came out of the liquor store.

There were three of them, a muscular, short-armed one, a weasly looking one, and the badass. Ashman didn't answer and walked east. He went down an alley, breaking into a trot after he turned. They followed him, running fast.

Ashman wanted, needed the fight. He put his package down and waited in the alley, crouched down, until they were just passing. Then he flew out silently behind them, choking out the slowest and yelling, "Stop!" as he pulled down the short-armed one.

The muscular one pulled a thick knife and the badass yelled, "Do it! Do it!" as he reached inside his jacket.

Ashman stuck a gun in each of their mean faces. "Go! Run away, Run away!" he yelled.

One ran, but the one with a hand in his jacket stayed. Ashman pointed his gun at the bad boy's heart and then extended his other arm so the muzzle of the second weapon was touching his left eye. "Do you want to die today, the day before Thanksgiving? You'll miss the parade," Ashman said, pulling back the hammers.

"Whatever," the badass said.

Ashman stepped a half step closer and nudged the mugger's jacket open with the barrel of one of his automatics. There was a Taurus .380 inside. Ashman took it and threw it away. It clattered on the sidewalk. "Run, run," he said.

When the badass did not move, Ashman pistol whipped him fast, knocking him to his knees. When he tried to get up, Ashman hit him twice more. Then he picked up his packages

and walked down Spruce Street, by the rich brownstones divid-
ed-up for dentists, newlyweds, and queers.

There were still plastic flowers at the Vietnam Memorial.
The fresh ones from Memorial Day had died and the dried ones
had blown away. The offerings of liquor and cartons of Lucky's
and Kools had long since been taken by people who had no
right.

Ashman walked to the names on the black wall, feeling eyes
on him from nearby or to the east. He unwrapped the whiskey
and after taking two drinks, walked the length of the memorial,
pouring the liquor to the fallen. He crossed over the overpass-
es to Delaware Avenue to watch the water.

Dewey's flagship, the Olympia, was there for three dollar
tours. Ashman went up on the cracking decks and stood for a
while in the light rain that blew in from the river. Afterwards,
he walked down Delaware Avenue, passing the closed sugar
refinery and pants factories. There were newly opened night-
clubs waiting for the riverboat gambling boats that would never
come. Ashman backtracked to the Society Hill Sheraton and
waited at the cab stand for a green and white taxi.

The Chase

Ashman took a yellow cab. As they headed down Delaware Avenue, he saw a green and white Victory pass by. The driver looked like the wispy haired one who had doped him. "Follow that Victory taxi," Ashman said.

"This ain't the movies, pal," his driver told him. "Where we goin'? I gotta log it in."

A twenty dollar bill got the driver to make a U-turn over the unused railroad tracks. He weighed three hundred pounds and wore a backwards Dallas Cowboy's hat. When traffic slowed or they had stopped for a light, he studied from a soft-backed dictionary, "Malani, Malaysia, Maldives," he once said out loud.

As they crossed Broad Street, he told Ashman, "Victory's giving his fare a real f-ing. Could've taken the cross-town."

"676?" Ashman asked.

"Yeah. He must know his fare's from out of town or some-thin'."

The two cabs got close at one point and Ashman could see a small man sitting behind the driver. The Victory, cab with Ashman after it, went out East River Drive and over the Falls Bridge.

The driver adjusted his hat. "You all right with this?" he asked.

"I'm all right. You all right?" answered Ashman. He passed him another twenty.

The driver touched his fingers to his hat in a salute. He shifted his huge body in his seat and seemed to spur his cab on by leaning forward.

They went out City Avenue, which was clogged with com-muters and cars pulling in and out of gas stations and fast food restaurants. The traffic thinned out as they approached Route 3.

"Used to be a Ford agency up here," the driver said. "Rudy Valentino's. Big deal. Rich guy. No munificence. Had it all, lost it all. My brother owned a jean joint across the street. Rich Rudy used to give my brother a raft of shit about parking. Well, you can see the jean joint's still there. Rudy went bankrupt and his wife ran off with the mechanic. We gotta break this chase off pretty soon. I'm not used to these sojourns. I gotta take a void."

"I don't want to lose him."

"I'll stop here at the Mobil Station. He'll have a stop light up ahead."

"I don't want to lose him," Ashman said again firmly.

"Affirmative," the huge cabbie answered. He pulled over and slid out of his seat. He was big everywhere and wore huge blue jeans with a belt and suspenders. He was out of the bathroom fast and pushed hard to catch the other cab. The road narrowed because of construction. Traffic was using the shoulder as the turning lane alongside the Montrose Cemetery.

"F-me. He's taking Bryn Mawr Avenue. My guess, he's taking him back to the Expressway," the cabbie said.

"The Expressway? It goes east or west from here?" Ashman asked him.

"West to Valley Forge. You can't get on east."

"Here's another twenty. Can you get to Valley Forge before they can?"

"Depends on traffic. His, I mean. We'll do fine. I'm Bobby. Call me Bobby, like the cops in England," the cabbie said. He tipped his backwards hat again.

Bobby pushed his way along in the passing lane and beat traffic as the light turned. By taking side roads and Route 23, he made Valley Forge in a little less than twenty minutes, about what it would take the Victory cab in medium traffic. Ashman directed him towards the Elms.

He wanted to make sure the green and white cab was going to the hospital, but he didn't want the cabbie to know of his interest. "A girls' school. It's a girls' school up there at the top of the hill."

"Nope," Bobby answered. It's actually some kind of rest

home or something, but for people who aren't right. It used to be a loony bin. You wanna go there?"

"I thought it was the girls' school, the junior college."

"Harcum, Parcum and Farkum," the driver laughed. "You used to be able to see that from the Expressway, its white pillars and all and some of the other buildings, but they built a hotel in front, The Riverview, although you can't see no river from it."

Ashman thought about the hotel where Lorraine had gotten blown up. Then he could see a green and white cab down below, going back East on the expressway. "He's down there," Ashman pointed.

"Sorry," Bobby said. "I lost them."

"Take me back," Ashman told him.

They went down the hill to 76 East the same way the green and white Victory cab was traveling, but far behind. When they were about half way in to the city, the cabbie reached under the seat and took out a stainless steel revolver and stealthily put it in his pocket. It looked like something he had done a thousand times.

"Things that bad?" Ashman asked him.

"Sorry," the cabbie said. "I hope you're all right with this. I got a permit." He accented the second syllable. "You come off the highway anywhere around here, you're in the badlands. The company don't know. They'd fire my ass. We all right?" he said, turning around. "We all right with this?"

"I didn't see a thing."

"So you'll do me the favor and not say anything? You know what I mean,"

"No problem." Ashman said. "No problem."

"Good deal, my liege. Good deal."

The cabbie tried to make it up to him. "You wanna hear the scanner? I got a police scanner. It keeps me from goin' nuts. Better than TV, and I can get around trouble. Knew a guy, in fact, he drove for Victory. Drove right into a shoot-out. Burglary at the steak house up on the Pike. Got himself shot."

"What's his name? I know a guy who drives for Victory," Ashman asked, trying for information.

"Doyle, I think. His name was Doyle."

"Doyle?"

"Yeah, Jack Doyle. He was flat on his back for a month. Then he stood home for a while. Moved to Queens. Got a job in the Lincoln Tunnel. You know, in one of them little booths. They only let them down for so long, like divers," he said. "Paid him for the full eight though." He stopped. "Am I talkin' too much? The wife, Marie, she says I talk too much. Maybe she's right. Nobody talks like us Eyetalians, yammering away the way we do."

They were in view of the city skyline when Ashman asked him to get off at Spring Garden Street. He wanted to make another pass at some cab stands and then at the train station at 30th and Market.

"You're the boss," said the cabbie.

Ashman had him drive down Arch street to the Convention

Center and then west on Market so he could see both cab stands. There were no green and whites. There a taxi stand for the shopper's, for Wannamakers.

"It's gone. I mean, it's not there no more."

"What's gone?" Ashman asked.

"Wanamakers. It's gone. So is Hecht's. So is Strawbridges. I mean, they're both Lord and Taylors or something. They're like appearing and disappearing right before your eyes."

"Drop me at 30th street," Ashman told him.

"Salutations and felicitations," Bobby answered, as he let him out. "I hope you find what you're looking for."

Ashman didn't answer, but smiled a smile that had no warmth. He was on the hunt and he had a trail to follow.

There was a long line of taxis that went from in front of the train station to the entrance on the other side. There were a number of Victorys there. Ashman walked around from the back of the line toward the front. The cabs were packed in so tight that Ashman knew if he found "Wispy," he had him.

He had no luck and went inside to call the number on the side of the cabs.

"Victory Cab," a woman with a Russian accent answered.

"I left my bag in your cab."

"Do you have the cab number?"

"No. He left me off in Valley Forge," Ashman said. "About a half hour ago. I'm a doctor."

"I'm sorry," she said. "Do you have any information?

Otherwise I will have to check their logs when they come in."

"No, only the driver was light haired, almost bald."

The woman thought it might be Alexi, but she knew that if somebody had left something in his cab, Alexi would have called it in. "I'm sorry, Doctor," she said. "If one of our drivers finds your bag, they'll call in."

"Is there a terminal?" Ashman asked.

"Only for some. Usually the drivers take their taxis home."

"Where are you? I want to come over. I have medicine in that bag. I was going to make a house call."

"We're behind the Burger King, across from the Terminal at 69th Street, Victory Avenue."

"I'll be there in a few minutes."

"Yes, Doctor," she answered.

Ashman wondered for a moment if he might be overdoing the cab thing. It didn't make sense that the guy who had grabbed him would still be driving a cab unless that was his deep cover or he was on another job. Maybe he wasn't the same guy. Maybe the black woman in the long green coat did him and he was fading out when the cabbie turned around. Or maybe they did it somewhere else and he was waking up in the taxi. But Ashman didn't think so. The flashback was too real.

When he got to the depot there were no cabs there. He walked over to the office. It was a one room stucco building with two metal desks and a tan sofa. Ashman wore a pair of glasses down on his nose and walked in without knocking.

"Doctor?" asked the Russian woman. She was in her sixties and had yellowish, waxy skin.

"Did my bag turn up?"

"No, I'm sorry. But I've been checking whenever they call in or I dispatch. Also, I checked my dispatch log. I didn't have anything to Valley Forge, but it could be under another destination. It's a shame you didn't get the cab number. Where did he pick you up?" she asked, lighting a cigarette which she held European-style.

Ashman knew any answer would be the wrong one. "This is very bad," he said He shook his head as he walked out.

He crossed the street and waited on a bench in the trolley terminal where he had a view of the entrance and exit of the taxi depot, but where he was out of the sight line from the office.

Wispy pulled up in his green and white. Ashman knew that any engagement would be good. If the cabbie ran, he would know it was him. If Wispy stayed, he would take and interrogate him.

He hailed the taxi and started for it. The cabbie pointed to the "off duty" sign on top of his cab, and drove away. Ashman limped after him for effect, knowing the cab was going to the depot.

He got to the depot only moments after Wispy, whose cab was the only one there. The hood was warm. It was number P828, but the number was badly faded.

Ashman wanted to get inside the cab and wait on the floor of the back seat. If he got caught, he would say he was looking for his bag. An old black man carrying cleaning tools got there first. Ashman withdrew.

The taxi driver came out to walk over to the Dunkin Donuts. He was about five foot, eight, on the thin side, maybe one hundred and forty pounds and wore cheap clothes. Ashman could see no weapon outlines at the shoulders, hips, or ankles. Wispy looked like a taxi driver , bad shoes, and polyester pants. His hair was very thin, his eyebrows almost non-existent.

"Okay, Moe," Wispy said to the black man, as he went for coffee. "Do your thing."

"Yessir," answered Moe. He took his bucket, sponge and the portable vacuum he had gotten from the depot and cleaned the cab. Ashman waited around the corner.

When the black man was done, the cabbie gave him a dollar and went to the depot to turn in his keys. There was a big hand written sign on the way in, "Always leave your vehicle Spick and Span for the Next Driver."

"Did you see the doctor?" the dispatcher asked him.

"The doctor? What doctor?"

"The doctor who left his bag in your car, on your run to Valley Forge?"

"No way. I always check the car."

"He said he left his bag," the dispatcher said.

"He's full of shit he said that," Wispy answered. He put his keys on the key board and went out back to get his car. Ashman followed close enough to catch him as he was getting in.

"This is a stick-up," Ashman told him. He put his gun to the taxi driver's neck.

"Don't shoot, don't shoot. I just turned my money in."

"I'm getting in up front," Ashman said. "Don't shit me. I will kill you."

"Don't, don't. I just cashed out. Here, here take my wallet, my watch," Wispy pleaded. He started for the wallet in his back pocket.

Ashman hit him hard on the wrist. "Don't reach for nothin'." Then he hit him in the face.

The cabbie moaned and covered up. He was bleeding and Ashman thought he might have pissed himself.

"We're going for a ride." Ashman told him. "I'm goin' to ask you some questions while you drive. If you give me the wrong answer or lie to me, I'm going to kill you. I'm going to shoot you in your throat so you'll bleed to death and choke on it. Drive with both hands on the wheel. What's your name? If you give me the wrong answer or lie to me, I'm going to kill you."

"O'Donnell, Eddie, Edward P.. O'Donnell, Edward Paul O'Donnell."

"Edward Paul O'Donnell, you ever see me before?"

"No, No, I don't think so."

Ashman hit him again. Edward cried out.

"I like this Edward P. What were you doing at The Elms Hospital in Valley Forge?"

"Took a fare," he answered with blood in his mouth.

"Who?"

"I don't know, I don't know, an old man. I think he was a doctor. He spoke with an accent. Says he left his bag, but he didn't."

"What kind of accent?" Ashman asked.

"I don't know."

"You been there before?"

"Once or twice, I think. Did I do something wrong?"

"Who'd you take?" Ashman asked, then feinted at him.

He thought for a moment, "Two women going to see a patient. Jews, by the way they were talking."

"Careful, Edward. Careful on this one. Who do you work for? If you get this wrong, you're dead."

"Statinsky. Max Statinsky."

"Who's he?"

"Statinsky. He owns the cab," the taxi driver answered.

"A Jew? Like those two women?" Ashman asked, trying to get Wispy talking.

"No, I wouldn't work for no Jew. Russian, though. He lives in Bala. He's a prick, but he's all right with me."

"Go on."

"He owns two cabs. Drives one himself."

Ashman raised his gun and cocked the hammer. "You see me before?"

The driver cowered.

Ashman knew he was getting nothing. "Gimmie your wallet and your watch," he demanded.

"Sure, sure," Edward P. O'Donnell said.

"Game's over," Ashman said. "I'm just a thief." He took the wallet and the watch. "Now, get out," he said.

Edward P. O'Donnell started running. Ashman drove away and left the car with the keys in the ignition.

Examinations

Major Kyle Lee Coates was to have Thanksgiving dinner at General Kendall's that afternoon, as he had the previous year. Last Thanksgiving there had been a number of heated discussions at the Major's dinner party, including one about Bosnia started by a Senator from New England. The Major thought the Senator was not only unable to hold his liquor, but was either gay or doing a good imitation of being so. Isabella Enchant, who again would be the Major's guest, was sufficiently convinced by the way that the Senator was admiring her bosom, that he was not gay in the slightest.

The Major had been told that Colonel Ari Bargai, retired Israeli Air Force, now at the Nitze School at John Hopkins, would be there this year, as well as someone from the National Defense University. If that turned out to be Ament, who had been so vocally critical of Somalia, there could be questions about a non-lethal weapon which had failed there.

Coates knew that any questions directed to him would likely be sharp ones. He spent the morning reviewing his reports, working until it was time to get ready for the general's party.

Isabella Enchant picked him up at just after two. She slid across the seat of her Jaguar to open his door, then pushed back the hood of her mink-lined aquamarine coat. He could smell her perfume come out in a wave.

"I do live in luxury," she said, caressing the mink lining. "Eddie Bauer is so anti-art." She gestured to his Bronco in the driveway. "And anti-art is anti-Christ. Don't you think so, Kyle?" She smiled. "You are beautiful in your uniform. How are you?"

"Charmed by you as always, Isabella. And you?"

"Right now, I am in a difficult period, Kyle, so quantum dimensional, so PKD." She repeated it as she backed out of his driveway without looking.

"That's always proved to be a problem for me as well Isabella, whatever it is," he said, arching his eyebrows "Especially before dinner with a general."

"Philip K. Dick, my beautifully committed Major. Have you time only for war and none for the universe? I must send you some of his writings. *Time Out of Joint* and the like, but only if you promise to ravenously devour them. Which reminds me, Helen does have a ravenous appetite herself, doesn't she?"

"Excuse me?" Ashman asked.

"Mrs. General, Helen. That's her name isn't it?"

"Helena," he corrected her.

"There's nothing 'Helena' about her. All 'Helen' if I ever saw one. I wonder if she'll color her hair to match her jewelry like she did last year. Do you like mine, by the way?" She took off a glove to show the ring that matched his eyes. "It's the General's secretary, you know," she added after a pause. "Helen's diddling him.".

"Simpson? He's got to be at least seventy, and besides he's a cripple."

"It's his cane," Isabella said.

"His what?" Ashman asked.

"That big, strong, heavy-headed cane," Isabella said, lighting a cigarette.

"Jesus, Isabella," he told her.

She laughed, sending the smoke out as she did.

The drive took almost two hours despite of the fact that Isabella held a constant speed of twenty miles per hour over the limit. He had offered to drive, but she insisted, adamant that she not arrive at such a fine dinner in the Major's "little truck." Isabella also repeatedly ignored his directions. "The road chooses us," she said.

The General's eighteen acre home, "The Orchard," had been in Mrs. Kendall's family since it was built in 1889 with a post-Civil War fortune. The furnishings included matching 16th Century German church pews which lined the center hall and an enormous gilded mirror framed by the outstretched wings of a giant eagle.

General and Mrs. Kendall and their guests had cocktails in

the library. Dinner was served in the formal dining room. The wall paper was hand-painted canvas celebrating the founding of West Point and the Battle of Yorktown.

The table sat twelve, although the seat closest to the patio door was always left empty. Simpson, the General's secretary, saw to the invitations, which included the General's daughter without a guest, Simpson himself, Major Coates, and his date. Attles was there from the State Department with his wife and as usual, a Senator or two were invited. Bargai attended again and this year, so did Mr. Fallon, who came in with the General and occupied the seat that last year belonged to Ament.

Dinner was well thought-out: quail, veal, sweet corn soufflé, Caesar salad, two kinds of squash, and raisin pie. The Major was relieved that Ament wasn't there and that the conversation was not about the failed NLW, but rather about the house. Mrs. Kendall went on about the wallpaper in the dining room. It was printed from wooden blocks which had been thought to be destroyed, she said, but were recently listed for auction at Sotheby's. *Better Homes and Gardens* had shown the wallpaper in the June "White House" issue. It also hung in a place called "Albemuth," but she hadn't seen that yet.

While Isabella and the other guests courteously listened or made genteel comments, the Major thought about the problems with his system. Orr had eighty-two kills in Vietnam and hadn't missed for him, except at Ashman. Something was wrong either with the weapon or, with Orr.

At dessert, Isabella told a vaguely anti-Semitic joke to Bargai. He responded to her in French that the trouble with gentiles is that they think all Jews are Jewish. Isabella smiled and repeated Bargai's answer in English for the Major, to which Fallon answered in German, "The trouble with the French is that they think everyone else is not."

"My, my," said Isabella. She turned to charm Fallon, but he seemed immune.

When the coffee was done, they moved outside to the patio for after-dinner drinks, cigars and serious discussion. "The knowledge warriors await us," Bargai said. "It is the management of information that shall bring victory. This is where it shall be decided."

Fallon agreed with him, "Our technology is better spent on such things than on the new weaponry, even Sikorsky's flying saucer helicopters or the so-called non-lethal weapons. Somalia eloquently demonstrates the superiority of information warfare. How much more powerful is the satellite broadcast of one nice young boy being dragged by a rope through the town square than a formation of tanks."

"Unless we cut off all their heads," the General said. He held his glass to the light, admiring his brandy. "Magnificent legs," he commented.

"Thank you," said Isabella.

The General laughed and drank her a toast. Then he gestured to the Major and the two of them walked out onto the flagstone path. "They are a bunch of sophists, Kyle," the General said. "They are 'self-aggrandizing careerists, cynically displacing principle among those entrusted with the steward of intelligence.'" The General looked at Major Coates, who couldn't place the quote. "Stephenson," he added.

"Excuse me?" the Major asked

"'Intrepid,' Sir William Stephenson, the superspy. William Stevenson, different spelling, wrote the book. He also said, the spy, not the author, 'Intelligence is the most important weapon.'"

"'Will democracies consent to their own survival?'" The Major added.

"Very good, Major."

"Not me, General. You said that last Thanksgiving."

"Oh yes, that was Intrepid, as well. Although it could have been the author Stevenson." The General changed tactics. "Make sure to chat with Mr. Fallon. You will be hearing from him on my behalf from time to time."

Coates nodded.

"Right enough," the General said. "On a more substantive issue, you shouldn't have given up on that sound to light project. The Israelis have it."

The Major needed to know more, but kept quiet.

"From there it got into the marketplace," General Kendall went on in soliloquy fashion, "There's such a thriving business nowadays. All the Soviet hardware and anything else you want. It's a supermarket.

"This situation does get a little sticky. The technology was used to take down Flight 800. One clean shot through the 747's superstructure. Renegade towelheads did the dirty deed. The Israeli's, Bet Shin, took care of them most expeditiously and with some drama." The general smiled and then continued,

"We assume the purpose of the act of terrorism was to point the accusing finger at the Israeli, 'Mene, mene tekel upharsim', the 'handwriting on the wall' or whatever. There would be little we could say since we've been equipping commercial airlines with surveillance doo-dads for the last year or so.

"Not to worry. It doesn't matter who shot down the TWA with what. It won't have happened a year from now." He finished his cognac and looked for a place to leave the class.

Our friends at the F.B.I. will deal with the issue of causation. The National Transportation Safety Board is as cooperative as always. There'll be as many possible explanations as there were dead passengers: It was a drone, it was a Navy missile, it was a bomb, it was the wiring of the fuel tanks. Boeing will take the blame and pay the freight. The whole situation will become forgotten, just good material for television shows.

"My only concern is that nobody knows that we had an option on the technology that knocked the plane down. That makes us look 'at fault' or inept. Both are quite bad."

The General offered Major Coates a cigar and they walked back in as the final coffee was being poured. The talk there was light and jovial and Major Coates tried to join in.

On the way home, Isabella picked a fight with him, Coates which was usually part of her foreplay, but he just had too much. "I'm chafed raw," he told her, and she let him off at that.

When they arrived at the Major's home, Isabella kissed him

on the cheek, then licked it. "I do miss you," she said.

"Me too. A raincheck, Isabella."

Major Coates remembered when the Israelis had beaten the Air Force to recover a Phantom jet in the Sinai, and then not only stole its state-of-the-art technology, but had it souped up and running in their planes in less than six months. The Pentagon and the State Department were livid. Careers were ended and lifetimes of service were lost to humiliation and shame.

He knew that there was a worse case situation facing him. If the Israeli weren't working on their own sound to light project, but had somehow utilized the NLW he had passed over, there would be a ton of bloody shit and it would all come downhill. Major Coates knew that his career would be in serious jeopardy if the lawyer, Greenglass, had passed their technology to Israel.

On the other hand, the Major thought, the Israelis might have been functioning completely independently. There was almost never anything unique about such projects. Sometimes new weapons were being pursued independently by two or three groups. Sometimes the weapons had been perfected long ago and were either put on the shelf or were being used invisibly.

Coates needed to find out what happened with the sonnoluminescence project he had rejected. If there were any problems or loose ends, they would have to be eliminated.

He thought about using Orr for that. Orr was deadly and except for that one miss of Ashman, he was the most reliable. The Major decided that he would find out quickly if Orr could be trusted.

He reviewed his files until after midnight. Afterwards, he thought about calling Isabella. Instead, he had a drink and smoked the last cigar of the day. Major Coates did not fall asleep easily.

* * *

Billy Orr was packing for an assignment in Detroit when his phone rang.

"I need to see you," the Major told him.

"When, sir?"

"Now."

Orr was confused. He had a 10:30 a.m. flight and the Major knew about his assignment. "I have a flight," he answered.

"It can wait."

"It will take me an hour to get there."

"My office in an hour," the Major answered.

Billy called the airport. There were flights as 2:30, 5:30 and one at 9 p.m., which would be an annoyance. He was able to get a seat on the 5:30 flight and changed his reservations so that he could meet with the Major and still complete his assignment.

It would take about forty minutes for him to get to the Advanced Research Project Agency. Orr left as soon as the reservations were made, taking his bags with him in case the meeting with the Major ran late. He left a note for his wife on the kitchen blackboard: "Leaving later. Back later. I'll call. Love, Bill."

The ride on the Beltway took longer than he anticipated. A

tractor trailer broke down in the center lane and disrupted everything around it. When Orr arrived at the Pentagon, the employees' spaces for ARPA were full, as were the next two floors in the garage. He wound his way up and parked on the roof. Taking the elevator down to the lobby, Orr presented his ID, and passed through to the other elevator that took him down to the Major's office.

"He's not in," the receptionist told him when he arrived. "Do you have an appointment? You're not in my book."

Billy Orr looked at his watch. He was on time. "Major Coates told me to come in. I'll wait."

He sat for a half hour. The receptionist took a phone call and then spoke to Orr, "The Major is running late. He asked me to give you this." She gave Orr a large manila envelope which he recognized as the type that initiated his annual testing, although that wasn't due for almost four months. He wondered whether the testing was the reason the Major called him and whether that meant there was a new assignment coming up.

Orr went down the hall to room 115 where the technician took his blood and urine, b.p., height, and weight. A tech he recognized from last time, gave him an EKG. Then he went into another room where a plump Korean woman administered psychological tests. That seemed to take longer than last year. Afterwards he went for his physical.

Dr. Rittenberg gave Orr a complete physical, including an orthopedic and neurological exam. The only things of note to the doctor were the increased crepitis in Orr's right shoulder and left elbow. "You still taking your Oruvail?" the doc asked him.

Orr nodded.

"Any stomach problems; pain, bleeding? The label says, 'Take with food, milk, or antacid,' but that's not enough. You still have a four percent bleed-out rate with any long-term non-steriodal anti-inflammatory, Oruvail, Orudis, Motrin, Advil. Take them with this." He wrote him a script for Cytotek. "How's your plumbing?" Rittenberg asked.

"I pee a lot."

"You get up at night?"

"Sometimes."

"You getting laid? Any problems?"

"That's okay."

"Well, I don't think it's anything." He looked at Orr's chart. "You're not due for a prostate screening. Use it or lose it. Don't tie your dick down." He wrote a room number on a slip of paper. "You're supposed to get an eye exam. See you next time."

Orr walked down the hall where another tech, this time one with a southern accent, gave him an eye exam. Afterwards, he took the elevator down to the range. Monty wasn't there. The new rangemaster was a smallish man with a large nose. His hair spiraled around his head.

"I'm the rangemaster today, Wolfang, Paul, P. People call me Paulie. I don't like 'Wolfie.' Monty is out. It says here I'm supposed to give you a 'comprehensive.' It'll take about two hours. Let's do this together."

Paulie gave Orr a Smith and Wesson model 640 and a 4013,

ears and glasses. "Standard stuff," he said. He went over the rules of the exam although Orr had heard them all before. Then they went out to the range. Orr noticed Gelman's sign was down.

"Yeah, everybody asks for it. It's being laminated," the rangemaster told him.

Orr shot a hundred rounds from the two handguns at still and moving targets and in the three situation rooms. After a break in which he had a soda and took a leak, he shot two rifles, a shotgun, and an AK. He washed up carefully, concerned that he was going on a job with all the residue on him. Orr was annoyed and his shoulder ached.

"Shoot straight," Paulie told him as he left.

"Right," Billy answered, "You too."

By the time Orr was getting off his flight in Detroit, the Major had the results of Orr's testing. He studied the raw test results and the conclusions drawn from them.

The psychological data and the profile drawn from it, confirmed a basically solid persona. William Orr had made an acceptable adjustment to his wartime experience, although he was somewhat "other directed." Orr identified strongly with the externals of God and Country. He was well centered, except that his self-worth depended on his performance. He was unlikely to leave any job undone. Orr had managed to come out of Vietnam with the social order of his mind intact. "He had his dignity and the cloak of his ideals remained in one piece," concluded Dr. Ho, who tended towards the poetic.

The Major reviewed the results of the physical testing and

their integration with the range results. He accepted the findings that Orr was compensating for the arthritis in his shoulder, and elbow. "Sniper's joints" they sometimes called it. That certainly would explain the errant shot.

Major Coates concluded that Orr's miss was not intentional, and that he would be an efficient tool in dealing with the NLW mess. The alternative conclusion would have put Billy Orr at the bottom of Lake Michigan.

Fallon

Major Coates began his plan for blocking any connection between the downing of Flight 800 and his sound to light project. Planning was the Major's greatest skill. He dissected the problem and analyzed the possible solutions with ferocious commitment.

He worked until dinner and went to the Republic. The Republic was a century-old gentleman's club, dedicated to those American noblemen who had served their Country and themselves.

Coates parked as usual in the adjoining open lot and came in the side door. Even in the side hall there was a doorman and a string of portraits.

"Good evening, Major," said John, the doorman, who knew all the members by their faces.

Coates nodded and walked in towards the center hall on the

thick blue carpet. When he got to his table, his drink was waiting. "The Way Things Should Be," he said to himself, repeating the Republic club's credo. He placed his order and lit a cigar.

The salad came soon, hearts of lettuce, tomato wedges, and circles of white onion. He ate as he sipped his drink. Then the steak arrived. It was small, but the center of it red as he had asked. The Major finished his meal, passing on the pie for dessert. He signed his check and sat in the reading room, smoking another cigar, and thinking about his plan.

At eight o'clock Major Coates left. John could see him coming down the long hall and called ahead for his car. The engine was running and the heat was on. The Major felt good. Sleep would end a productive day. The car phone rang. He hoped it was Isabella.

"This is Fallon. Meet me in your office in an hour."

"Channels?" Coates asked.

"I don't think you want anybody there," Fallon told him.

Coates thought about calling the Trouble Officer on duty at the Pentagon, but then realized he was probably overreacting. Most likely, Fallon was delivering a message from General Kendall.

Nevertheless, the Major as always, took precautions. He thought of coming late to meet Fallon on the way out, but it would give him a greater advantage to be there waiting. By changing his route and pushing it, he was at his office almost twenty minutes early.

There was nobody logged in for his office or his floor when the Major got to the security officer's deck. But when he got off the elevator and came around and down the hall, he could see that there was a light on in his office. He slid the safety off his weapon.

Major Coates went into his office almost at a dash and at an acute angle. No one was there. Nothing looked out of place. He was wary but annoyed. "I don't like being played with," he said out loud.

The Duty Sergeant came up, checking his route, "Everything square, sir?" he asked the Major.

"Yes, Sergeant. I'll be here just a few more minutes. Please check back in a quarter of an hour."

The Major waited for fifteen more minutes. When the sergeant came back to his office as directed, Coates left for his car. It was parked in his space in a secure lot and had a state of the art security system. Fallon was waiting in the passenger's seat with the dome light on. He turned his hawk-like face towards the Major as he got in.

"Make yourself comfortable," the Major told him. "I'm not surprised and I'm not amused."

"I'd like a chat," Fallon answered, smiling.

"I thought you people at the National Defense University were academics."

"I'm not NDU."

"Fine, Fallon, you're not NDU and you're in my car."

"I'm not Fallon."

"What do you want?"

"We'd like to clear up something," Fallon told him.

"We?"

"I'm here on behalf of General Kendall."

"Then why all this nonsense? You are either Fallon or you are not. If you wish, you can tell me what you have to tell me or you can get out of here. In either case, I'll be seeing the General tomorrow about this annoying charade."

"Of course, you're not going to be seeing General Kendall tomorrow, Major. The General will be unavailable to you until Flight 800 calms down. I believe that he already told you that he doesn't wish to look at fault, or inept. Let's go for a ride and talk."

"We'll do it here." The Major paused and spoke slowly, "I don't want this to get complicated and I don't like fencing."

Fallon opened his window a bit. The Major took that for a signal and changed his posture. "You needn't reach for your weapon, Major Coates," Fallon told him. "You really are being quite paranoid."

Coates did not move.

"It's all so vulgar," Fallon went on. "What I'm here about. But really what can one expect from those with their 'strong ethnic ties.' I mean the Israelis of course."

The Major knew Fallon was talking about the sonnolumi-nescence project. He wondered whether this was an extension of General Kendall's conversation or a new one.

Fallon went on, putting a mint in his mouth. "We have run checks on everybody you've ever met, Major. That normally would be sufficient, but we're understandably aggressive with the Israelis, who of course, define the word 'aggressive' even before their little spy, Jonathan Pollard. Dear bar mitzvah boy should have stuck to selling dry goods or corned beef or whatever.

Everybody comes up fine, except now and then. Like our Israeli friend, Bargai. He's been working on and off for the British since 1993, and believe it or not, the French once or twice," Fallon looked for a reaction, but Coates gave him none. "Anyway, this sound-light thing. It's done with mirrors, literally. Interferometers. You know what they are?"

Fallon answered himself, "Interferometers are series-linked mirrors that electronically connect light waves. The output is boosted dramatically in a very compact space.

We're concerned about any possible connection between the NLW group you passed over and the Israelis. The Jews were nice enough to clean-up the terrorist cel that pilfered their technology and took down the 747. We expect you to clean-up any mess that you might have left behind."

Fallon got into the Crown Victoria that pulled up. As it was pulling away he opened his window. "Dakkas works for us," he said. "Have a pleasant evening."

As soon as Fallon left, Coates dictated a detailed memo of what had happened, including Fallon's license plate number, even though he knew that it would prove of no help. He included all the things he had noted about Fallon, an expensive overcoat, likely Brooks Brothers, a thin platinum wedding ring, and a steel-cased watch. Fallon's pants legs were wide below the knee and he sat with his left leg forward. He was probably wearing an ankle rig. Excellent dental caps, a Pelican pen in his pocket, a hint of aftershave, the mints. There was a scar on the second knuckle of his right hand. When he got out of the car and into the Crown Victoria, he moved with no particular grace or muscularity. His approach and little jokes, including or not about Bargai or Dakkas, were unnecessary and showed either boredom, or over-confidence. The driver of Fallon's car looked military.

Coates knew what his assignment was, but he also knew that he had been given it twice, once by General Kendall and now by Fallon. This meant that he had two assignments: to back-track on the sonnoluminescence project and now, to find out about Fallon.

If Fallon was one of ours, the Major thought, he was either working directly for General Kendall or for the Defense Technical Security Administration. The Major also considered that Fallon was not one of theirs. If he was a bogey, he would most likely be Israeli, MOSAD, or Bet Shin. The Major had good contact at the Joint Intelligence Community Staff, "The Boys on G Street," they called themselves, and they would know who Fallon was working for.

Major Coates wondered who else might be involved with Fallon. Orr had passed all his tests. Was Dakkas a threat? Ashman? Someone on other projects? Someone who was involved for reasons he didn't yet know of?

Major Coates opened his window and lit a cigar, inhaling the first bit of smoke. He would attack the Fallon matter and was confident that he would figure it out.

Coates went to see Isabella. He had already done his due

diligence on her living conditions. The building had been con-
verted to a duplex. Isabella lived on the second floor. The
owner lived on the first floor and worked for the American
Parrot Association. He was a widower. His daughters visited
him on occasion.

The Major had a key that Isabella didn't know about, but he
didn't use it. He could hear her big cat, Pinky Tony, running to
the front door in response to his buzz.

"Go away," Isabella called into the intercom. She played
her ferociously barking guard dog tape.

"It's me," he said.

"So am I," she answered as she let him in. She was wearing purple fishnet tights and a San Jose Sharks tee shirt.

"I am asleep, Yoshihiro," she told him. She went into the
kitchen shuffling her feet. "I am wearing white flannel
trousers," she said. Her black hair was tied up in red and purple ribbons. "We cannot eat. Can we talk tomorrow?" she
said. "Come to bed, my Paladin," Isabella told him. She
smelled like old wine as she came close. The cat paced back
and forth for the birds on the first floor.

The Major sat on Isabella's bed and called Dakkas at home.
He needed to know whether or not Dakkas was working for
Fallon and if so, were they all on the same side. Major Coates
was confident that he would be able to tell by meeting with him.

"Yes?" Dakkas answered.

"I don't like this," Coates told him.

"Major?"

"I don't like this."

"Sir?"

"I'll see you tomorrow, Emil. I don't know what your additional duty is, but we'll see tomorrow."

Major Coates hung up and turned to Isabella, who was made singing sounds and then crying sounds as she opened for him.

Dakkas came up from the kitchen where he had taken the call. He was angry. "I gotta go tomorrow morning," he told her.

They had breakfast plans for the next day, but Sophie was understanding, "Be back by noon. We can go to brunch," she told Emil.

"I hope so," he answered.

"Can you pick Sonny up?" she asked. "The Karenty's are going to his parents' for the weekend."

"I'll try. If not, I'll call. I'll call anyway. If you don't hear from me by eleven-thirty, you'll have to get her. You need anything?"

"Just you," she answered.

The big dog came over and nuzzled her. "He's sliming me!" Sophie complained.

"Down!" Emil said. He took the dog outside and walked around their square yard, staying outside longer than usual as he tried to figure out what was going on. When Dakkas came up to bed, Sophie was asleep.

He didn't sleep well and woke-up twice. Each time, he

walked down the hall and checked on Sonny. The Great Dane stirred on his bed at the top of the stairs and went back to sleep.

Emil got up early and drove down to the high school track and ran before breakfast. Sonny slept late, so he and Sophie had some time together before he had to leave. She wanted to make love, but he was resentful from the night before.

"How about a back rub?" she asked him.

"Sure," he told her. Dakkas thought about the Major as he lay there. He was angry that the Major had questioned his commitment and was wary that there was something else going on.

"Who are you working for?" the Major asked Dakkas when they met.

"Sir?"

"Who are you working for?" he asked again.

"You, sir. ARPA."

"Who else?"

"My Government. My Country."

"Who else? Emil, who else? DIA? CIA?"

"No, sir."

"NJI? FBI?"

"What's going on here, Major?" Dakkas asked. He shifted his weight a bit.

"NSA? DISA?" The Major asked.

Dakkas became more and more agitated.

"You don't like this, Emil?"

"No, I don't, sir."

"Orr?" the Major asked as he picked up his cigar clipper.

Dakkas watched his hands move. "Or what?" he asked.

"Orr, your brother-in-law."

"I don't..."

"Ashman? Maya Charcot?'

"Who? Look, Major, I don't..."

"The General?" Coates paused longer between each. "Fallon? Karenty?"

Dakkas stood up. "Pardon me, sir, but you and everybody else keep my family out of this!"

"Is that a threat, Emil?"

"You're fucking right it is, sir, talking about my daughter's friend means talking about my daughter."

"Duly noted, Dakkas. Sit down," Major Coates told him.

Dakkas didn't move.

"My apologies. Please sit down."

Major Coates turned on the gray plastic air cleaner on his desk and when the fan was whirring, he lit his cigar, sending the smoke over to the left and behind him where it was sucked up by the machine.

Dakkas sat down with his hands on his thighs and his legs spread apart. The Major noticed that he was toward the front of the chair, positioned so that he could launch an attack.

"Relax, Emil."

"Not hardly, sir, with that crack about my family, my daughter's friend, and all. What is this? Some kind of a test?"

"No test. Except where you and Fallon are concerned."

"And just who is that?"

The Major passed him an envelope containing the data he had on Fallon, the photo, his memo, the license plate number. He held back any information about Fallon working for General Kendall. "Get concerned Emil. He might be anybody. My guess is he's either 'No Such Agency' or 'Santa's Helpers', if he's one of ours at all. I'll take care of any non-domestic issue."

"Who are they, sir?

The Major looked at him, "No such Agency, Fort Meade."

Dakkas looked at him like he still didn't understand.

"No Such Agency is NSA, The National Security Agency."

"No, not them, the other one."

"'Santa's Helpers' are DITSA, Defense Technical Security Administration. They watchdog new toys. In any case, his Crown Vic started out for the Dulles Airport, so start there. That's where the National Reconnaissance Office is."

"Or, he was catching a plane, Major."

Coates ignored that, "He says you work for him. If you do, Emil, you're going to have a hell of a job disproving it. I want you to shadow him and any of his people, including yourself if you're in on it," he said, smiling. "I want everything."

"Is there an 'or else,' Major?" Dakkas asked.

"There's always an 'or else.'"

"My family, Major? Because then we have a problem."

Major Coates had taken a bag of pistachio nuts from his desk. Dakkas watched his hands move.

"Just Orr, your brother in-law. He's going to be shadowing you." The Major pried the nuts apart with his thumb and forefinger. "You have a week. Now get back to your holiday. I'm sorry to have interrupted you." Then he added, "And your family."

Dakkas got up and left. The Major wanted them all in the same basket. He would put Dakkas on Fallon, Orr on Maya Charcot, Ashman on Dakkas and Dakkas, Orr, and Ashman on each other. He cleared the oily residue of the nuts from under his nails with his pocket knife and made some notes.

Major Coates did his own intel on Fallon and came up with nothing, which meant he'd either have to get the answer from the Joint Intelligence database or the people he had put on the job would have to come up with something.

Maybe one of his people, Dakkas, Orr, or Ashman would trip over something or catch someone covering up. He would give his efforts a week and then, if he had nothing, he'd have to go to General Kendall with it. That was something he did not want to do in light of his recent problems with the sonnoluminescence.

Coates emptied his ashtray and turned off his air cleaner. Then he drove back to Isabella's, calling her from his car.

The phone rang nine times before Isabella's tape picked up. "This is Isabella," it said, "I am here, but there. Shantih, shantih, my darlings." Then there was a long pause and she laughed, "Your call is non-local."

He used his key to get in. He could hear the German shepherd tape as he came up the steps. The big cat ran up as he opened the door, but the apartment was empty, no furniture no Isabella Enchant, nothing.

Greenglass

Major Coates began another evaluation of the sound to light project. He already had everything he needed on Fulliard Stevens. Stevens was exactly what he appeared to be, a black posture wrapped in gray flannel and now quite dead. There was nothing in his background or activities that indicated that he had direct or indirect contact with the Israelis or would do so.

Coates was similarly convinced that other than her involvement with Ashman, Maya Charcot was nothing in the equation. He had checked her background completely, which was in addition to what he considered his own excellent judgment of women.

The Major's data on Switt indicated that he grew up outside of Boston and went to the University of Chicago for his undergraduate degree and his doctorate. He had no military, taught two semesters at Mount Holyoke and then a year at Bucknell.

Switt was married to a music therapist he had met in college and they had a one daughter. He had been arrested once in college at a sit-in at a nuclear facility. No other politics. He was a registered Democrat.

Switt's field was fluid mechanics. He had published a number of times. Each of the articles and all co-authors had been scanned and cross-referenced with all open and closed NLW projects and key names. One of the co-authors of one of Switt's articles went to undergraduate school with Greenglass and one was Israeli.

Major Coates had already secured the follow-up information on the co-author who went to school with Greenglass. She had died of leukemia two years ago. The Israeli was a dead-end also.

Switt's tax returns didn't show anything out of the ordinary. He had a thirty year mortgage he was in the process of refinancing, a 1991 Volvo wagon, and a financed Saturn two-door. The Major already had screened Switt before their restaurant meeting and they had met face to face there. Switt was nothing.

Attorney Martin Greenglass was next. Major Coates reviewed the intelligence he had gathered. Martin Greenglass was forty-seven years old and had gone to college at Syracuse, where his grades were fair, and then to Brooklyn Law School, where he met his first wife. He had no armed services. No real problems, except two disciplinary problems at Syracuse for rowdy behavior and two speeding tickets, one of which he took to trial and had dismissed. Greenglass was involved in politics on the most local level and only where it aided his business.

His first wife, Marci Sokolow, taught second grade and had put him through law school. They were divorced two years after he passed the Bar exam, which he did on his first attempt. She remarried a pharmacist. Greenglass married Maureen O'Reilly, and they had two daughters, Marla and Elizabeth. Her cousin's brother was a med tech at the Pentagon. The Major inputted a memo to have that checked again.

Greenglass worked for the Suffolk County D.A.'s office after he was admitted to the Bar. No problems, nothing relevant about his caseload. He stayed two years and then went to work for Leibovitz and Abraham, a Brooklyn general practice firm, doing personal injury work. No complaints with the State Ethics Board. Two years later, he opened his own firm, Martin H. Greenglass and Associates. He had no associates at first, although he had two now. He had ads in three local phone books.

The most recent corporate tax returns showed that his firm grossed between three hundred and fifty thousand dollars and a half million dollars the last two years. Martin took out two hundred thousand each year. His wife made fifty two thousand dollars teaching at the Daley Elementary School. They had minimum interest income.

The cross-referenced property and lien search showed a four bedroom Georgian colonial home, on a little over a half an acre with an eighty percent mortgage, and a vacation home in Calicoon, New York. The financing on the Calicoon property was by a mortgage of one hundred seventy five thousand dollars and a down payment of seventy five. That mortgage was sold twice and then assumed by Bank Hapolomin, whose mortgage was paid off two weeks ago. The recent cancellation of the large debt by an Israeli bank was cause enough for the Major to pay lawyer Greenglass a personal visit.

"The Law Offices of Martin H. Greenglass and Associates. May I help you?" answered the receptionist, Marie Castrovillo. She interrupted her doodling in the margins of her message pad to take down the caller's name.

"My name is John Hall." Major Coates told her. "My daughter was hurt in a car accident."

"Just one minute," the receptionist told him. She rang Mr. Greenglass, but his line was busy. Then she tried each of the associate attorneys and Mr. Greenglass' secretary as she had been directed. The secretary took the call.

"This is Carol, Mr. Greenglass' secretary. I understand your daughter was involved in an automobile accident," she told the caller.

"On Thursday. Her name is Babette. Where's the lawyer?" he answered.

"Do you have insurance, Mr. Hall?" she asked.

"We both do. Am I going to get to speak to a lawyer?"

"Mr. Greenglass is not available at the moment, but I'd be happy to take your information."

"She broke her leg. Two lawyers have called already today. If he wants the case, it has to be today. I can only come in after five when I'm done my shift, " the Major told her. "And I'm not talkin' to no secretary."

After looking at her boss's schedule, Carol made the appointment. He had to be at a six o'clock zoning meeting.

"Mr. Greenglass will meet with you personally, today. Please be on time," she said. "I'm squeezing you in."

"Sure, sure," Major Coates answered her. "I'm the one with the case."

Greenglass buzzed his secretary after he concluded his phone call to Marvin Husfeldt, who had the zoning problem that was coming to a first hearing that evening.

"Who was on 'three'?" he asked his secretary.

"A 'P.I.' case, Mr. Greenglass. A broken leg. Insurance," she answered.

"Did we get it? Somebody else take the call?"

"I did, Mr. Greenglass. He's coming in at five." She anticipated his concern about his schedule. "You'll still be able to make the zoning meeting."

"Good, good," Greenglass told her.

The lawyer went over his notes from the Husfeldt call and his call to the attorney who represented Husfeldt's partner. That call lasted ten minutes. He recorded 0.4 hours in Husfeldt's bill for review of file and a 0.3 for each call, 0.3 for the notes he took, which were billed as a "memo to file," and 0.4 for research — 1.7 hours for twenty-five minutes work. The joy of time, he thought.

Mark Mesirov, who was a second year associate, stood in the doorway, waiting to be noticed.

"Mark, Mark, What is it? Use the intercom."

"It was busy, Mr. Greenglass. You told me to see you when

TUNNEL RUNNER | 181

I was done reviewing the Release."

"Well?"

Mesirov fiddled with his watch chain. "I did. I think it's acceptable."

"Let me see," said Greenglass. He took the paper from him. "Did you review the Joint Tortfeasor Act? It seems to me it's only 'acceptable' for the insurance company. It seems to me that when I go against the second vehicle, they're going to hit me over the head with this Release, and I'm going to be sued and then you're not going to have a job here." He paused, "Or anywhere else. I'll tell everybody you were stealing and I caught you trying to whack-off on the copy machine. Go fix it. We want a dollar for dollar set-off. I need it by tomorrow at ten, no, nine o'clock tomorrow morning."

Mesirov stood there waiting for further instructions. The intercom rang and Greenglass waved him away and picked it up.

"'You told me to remind you when it's 11:30," Carol told him.

Greenglass answered, "Right, right." He took his pill and then went over the papers for the zoning hearing scheduled for that night. Connestoga Printing needed zoning approval for an extension to its loading zone. The company was on a lease-purchase with an option to buy, which it would assert only if it got the zoning approval for the loading dock. The neighbors were against the extension because it would cut into an adjacent public parking lot. The opposition was vocal, but weak. Greenglass was sure he could get a large fee and the zoning approval.

"The mail's in," Ms. Castrovillo told him when he picked up her page.

It was one of "The Five Immutable Rules" which were laminated and taped to the receptionist's desk: One: "Always take a caller's name and phone number: Two: "Always ask what the call is regarding;" Three: "If Mr. Greenglass is not in, always give the call to his secretary;" Four: "If the call is regarding an accident case, make sure that someone takes the call." Five: "Always buzz him, or his secretary if he is not in, <u>the moment</u> the mail arrives."

When Attorney Martin Greenglass got back to his office at 5:10 from an outside meeting, he discovered that Mr. John Hall had not arrived. By 5:30 he knew the auto accident was gone, likely bought by the competition.

Greenglass changed into a clean white shirt for the zoning hearing and locked-up. He'd eat afterwards and call home from the car. When he went out to the parking lot, he saw Major Coates leaning against his green Lexus. The Major was wearing a trench coat and sunglasses. The appearance was enough to make the lawyer's heart race.

The Major beat him to the first words, "This is official business"

Martin Greenglass had been bullied before and knew well enough to fight back even against the Federal Government. "I do not do official business in a parking lot, or after hours," he said. "If you wish to speak to me, Mr. Hackett, although I have no idea about what, you may call during business hours."

The attorney felt better having taken the offensive, but he was confused and there was a lingering fear. He had met this man only once before and that deal went nowhere. He hadn't violated any rules, unless there were some he didn't know about. That gave him a sinking feeling in his stomach. He hoped it didn't show.

"I am not Mr. Hackett and I am not Mr. Hall. If you make me come back, I won't be alone and you won't like that." When Major Coates saw the lawyer slump, he knew he had him, "This is not about you," Coates said, smiling, "but it has to be resolved tonight. It will take about a half hour. It is extremely important to your Country and will not be postponed."

"I've a zoning hearing at six," Greenglass answered. He felt silly when he said that.

"We can meet afterwards," The Major paused. "For a drink."

While this somewhat calmed Greenglass, his mind still raced. He wondered what he had done wrong, what this was all about, and how he could get out of it. He looked at his watch. "Where?" he asked.

"Your usual," Coates answered.

"Excuse me?"

"The Angus, Route 30."

The lawyer was stunned, but agreed and was glad to get away to the zoning hearing. He called home from the car. His wife could tell there was something in his voice, "Everything all right, hon?" she asked him.

"It's the zoning hearing, business," he told her. "You alright right? The girls?"

Greenglass thought about running away, but took a deep breath. He knew he couldn't run and he knew that he was clever. He'd do the zoning hearing and then the meeting with the man in the trench coat, whatever that was about. Maybe he'd have somebody there for security and as a witness. He called the private investigator he used in his law practice, but got the answering service instead and told them that it was urgent.

Fat Marvin Husfeldt was at the borough hall with his check. Greenglass thought he looked like a tuna in clothes. They were third on the zoning list. The Tookenay Civic Association was there, which meant at least two more hearings, and a nice fee. The demands of the moment distracted him from thinking about the man in the trench coat, and he was glad for it.

The Chairman of the Zoning Board was a large moon-faced man. He asked if there were any protesters. When they stood up, he called out "Contest," and motioned Greenglass and the president of the Civic Association to the table in front of him. Husfeldt started over, but Greenglass gestured him back.

"You are best advised to retain counsel," the chairman told the Civic Association. He looked at the schedule. "Hearing continued for thirty days. Next case."

"Too bad, Marvin," the attorney told his client. "It looks like we're going to have our hands full."

Greenglass tried his P.I. again from his carphone, but with no success. This made him think about not going to the meeting, but the image of the Major convinced him otherwise.

He got to the restaurant ten minutes early and was relieved that no one was watching for him. Greenglass thought that now he would at least have time to prepare himself for the meeting or get to his investigator. Hopefully, there would be no meeting at all.

"The usual, Mr. G?" the waitress asked him. She was round-faced with a large mole that went partially on to her upper lip.

"Thanks," he said. The drink would settle him down. He'd wait fifteen minutes.

The drink arrived and the Major didn't. Greenglass finished his scotch and thought about another. He looked at his watch. It was seventeen minutes after. He'd take a leak, pay the check, and leave.

The lawyer was at the urinal when the Major took him by the feet. Greenglass grabbed the fixture for balance and cried out. His tie and jacket went into the toilet and his chin slammed againsth the porcelain as the Major dragged him backwards into a stall. Greenglass was bleeding and it smeared on the tile floor.

There was no time to struggle. Before he knew it, Greenglass was gasping for breath with the Major sitting on his chest and pressing a heavy black gun into his eye.

"Hello, Attorney Greenglass," the Major said, cocking the hammer on his .45. "I'm not who you think I am, but rather who you should think I am. I am the Israeli Central Institute for Intelligence and Special Missions. I am going to ask you two questions. If you give me the wrong answers, I'm going to kill you. If you lie to me, I'm going to kill you."

The lawyer's eyes were bulging and he had trouble breathing. There was blood in his mouth. The Major pushed the muzzle of the gun against the lawyer's forehead. Greenglass started to shake.

Major Coates smiled. "The two questions are: One: Who arranged the loan pay off to Bank Hapolomin? And, Two: Who did you give the plans to?"

Martin Greenglass could only think about his mortgage. It didn't make any sense. He had paid off the loan from a settlement of his own personal injury claim, rear ended on Riverside Drive. He paid the mortgage with the settlement check. There weren't any plans, unless he meant the plans for the rehab of his office building.

First he couldn't talk. Then he stammered, "For the house? For my building? For...."

"No," said Coates, pushing his knee into Greenglass' throat.

Greenglass was ashen and grasping for breath. "My auto case. I paid the bank with that. Please," he said and started to cry.

The Major was satisfied that the lawyer knew nothing, and that the NLW group had not sold their technology to the Israelis. "Clean yourself up, counselor," he said as he left. "You look a mess. Shalom."

Home

Dr. Charcot awoke at the sound of cooking. Then she realized it was the television. She looked at her watch, shut it off, and tried to fall back asleep, turning to the wall and wrapping her feet in the blanket. It was a quarter to four in the morning. She drifted on the edge of sleep.

When Maya awoke again, she could hear noise from downstairs. Although it was Thanksgiving morning, the favored customers came in to pick up their fresh-killed turkeys and odds and ends to start the long day's cooking.

Two of the Laotians came by to get cigarettes, but Hugey waved them away, "Closed, youse two monkeys." He looked over to Rosie, who had come downstairs for some pimentos, "I don't know whose worser, them squattin' gooks or Tyronne."

"Them guys?" she said. "Gimme them any day over Tyronne, except for them tong gangs. But don't they look like birds, Hugey, the way they sit out there on the sidewalk."

When Rosie looked outside, she saw Ashman through the spaces in the flattened-out cardboard that they had put over the window. He saw her seeing him, but kept walking up the block, past Dixie Street and into the parking lot at St. Theresa's. Father Dominic was sweeping up the cigarette butts, beer cans, and the condoms, which had started appearing like washed-up sea creatures.

Ashman walked around the corner and came down Rosie's block from the other end. He didn't remember the Asians being there before and he didn't like them. He went right at them and they scattered.

Venudo had told Rosie that Ashman was coming. She opened the door for him. "Hey," she said.

"Hey," Ashman answered.

Hugey looked up from washing the turkeys and rubbing them with garlic. He wasn't sure who Ashman was, except that he sounded like he was a friend of Rosie's. "How youse doin?" he asked.

"How youse doin?" Ashman answered.

"Good, good," Hugey said.

Rosie was going back through the store to go back upstairs when there was another knock on the glass door. "I'll get it," she said. It was Jimmy Two Plates. Ashman moved behind one of the stacks of shelves.

"Pack of Lucky's, two packs," Rosie told Hugey when she saw who it was. Hugey took them out of the metal rack over the counter. Ashman came back out and looked at the tomatoes and mushrooms.

Hugey held up one of the turkeys by its legs. "This OK, Mr. Gigante? Good breast. Nice laigs."

The old man leaned forward so he could see. "That's nice," he said.

"Good, Mr. Gigante. We'll bring it by."

"Goin' to my daughter's in Broomall. They're pickin' me up."

"That's a good thing," Rosie added.

Mr. Gigante went back out, adjusting the brim of his hat.

"Jimmy Two Plates?" Ashman asked.

"He's got nothing to do," she answered.

"Except die, Rosie."

"That's a lot," she answered.

"Sometimes it's not enough," Ashman told her.

"You're here at the right time," Rosie said when they got upstairs. "Your lady's unhappy. Bored. 'Onwey' she called it, whatever that means."

"'Ennui.' It means she is going to be a pain in the ass."

"It's good you're here. I'd've had to jack her," Rosie said laughing.

"She awake?"

"I don't know. I checked on her when I got back from my

shift. She was snoring like a baby. Second door down the hall. Stevie left. You just missed him."

Ashman didn't like that. That meant that for a time, it was just Rosie. The guy behind the counter didn't count. That wasn't good. "Complacency can bring-on a lot of death," Ashman said outloud, but Rosie didn't hear him.

He went down the hall and looked in Maya's room. She had the covers cocooned around her and was facing the wall. She was asleep, but when he got into bed she turned towards him.

"I'm glad you're here," Maya said. "My iron soldier come home."

Ashman went into the covers held open for him and she dozed with her head on his chest. "You have to get up soon," he told her.

"No," she answered.

"The parade."

"I'm not going," Maya told him.

"You always go."

"I'm not going. I'm still dreaming."

"Fifteen minutes," Ashman said. He let her fall back asleep and watched her.

After Maya showered and dressed, they walked to breakfast and then to the other side of the park. Maya wanted to hold hands, but Ashman wouldn't. He walked arm in arm with her which comforted her, but still allowed him to push or turn her and to get to his weapon.

When they got to the parade route, both sides of the road were lined by early watchers. Maya lit her cigarette and was catching clouds of menthol smoke as she waited for the waves of drummers and marching bands to come down from around the hill.

Ashman could hear the parade sounds from a long way off. Having "wolf ears" was a hunter's necessity, but some of the best he knew could not turn that down. They could hear keys or steps or the turning of a page as loud as sound effects in a microphone. They leapt at the closing of a door.

The marchers with their white drums and horns and the young girls with white batons came marching down the hill. Ashman looked past them and into the crowd. He could not view any situation without looking for danger. He saw Nash's face in the crowd. The little man was jumping up and down.

The faces near Nash were not familiar, Downes faces with Asian eyes and ones with vacant stares and drooling men, holding hands like toddlers. Ashman looked for a man smoking a cigar. He memorized the people closest to Nash and then further out, until more parade came down and separated them. Police on horseback came by, followed by the floats and things he had seen as he came up from the train tunnel the day before.

Ashman told Maya that he was going to buy her one of the silver balloons that were waving on strings across the street. He made his way through the crowd so he could look for the Elms van and take the license plates of the cars next to it. Perhaps one of them would belong to the cigarman.

Major Coates came up to him from the right. "Op sec," the Major said.

Ashman had his hand on his gun inside his windbreaker and he turned it before he turned his face. "Good morning, Major," he said when he saw who it was.

"Let's walk and talk," Coates answered him.

Ashman followed the Major across the street, keeping his finger on the trigger guard. They went down into the doorway of Doroshow's Drugs.

"You have no secure phone," the Major said.

Ashman knew that was bullshit, but said nothing.

"Fallon," the Major went on. "You know him?"

"Charlie, Charlamagne Fallon is dead," Ashman told him, "a long time ago."

"No, Find him," said Coates. He handed Ashman an envelope with all the information he had collected on the man who had appeared in his car. "Maybe DTSA or NSA. He's most likely ours, but maybe not. Dakkas works for him. Dakkas is on you. So is his partner, Orr. Follow them. Find Fallon."

When the conversation was over, Major Coates left. He wondered again about Ashman. He had thought about planting listening devices at Maya's, but knew that even if Orr planted double taps and decoys, Ashman would find them. Instead, the Major relied on the National Reconnaissance Office, which maintained long range surveillance. He would use that agency to provide intel on Ashman, Dakkas, and Orr. The Major knew that he dared not approach the NRO about Fallon, who could be in their employ.

Maya enjoyed the parade, but was glad to get home that

evening. She was on her porch, watering her plants and dusting their leaves. "My plants look like shit," she said. "We
were away too long." She came in from the porch to fill up her
white enamel spritzer and the copper watering can. "The place
geraniums go to die," she told Ashman. "But I'm glad we're
here."

"Don't water them too much," he answered.

"I don't like these times."

"Do you feel all right?"

"I'm fine. I don't like these times. I don't like it when my
life is this way." She went on when he didn't say anything, "Is
it me?" She was frightened and confused. Ashman had told her
not to worry. However at the parade Maya thought she had
seen him with Hackett, the government contracting officer who
had seen their project.

"I told you no one was interested in you that way," Ashman
told her.

"Never mind," she said. "I'm sorry. I know I get things out
of order. I make things up."

"I forgive you," he said.

"About what?" she asked.

"About everything," he answered.

"About everything?"

"Yes," he said, "Here or there. Now or then. Known or
unknown." But even while Ashman was telling Maya that he
was forgiving her, he trusted no one. "What's wrong?" he

asked her quietly.

"Nothing's wrong that shooting up the kitchen wouldn't cure." Maya looked out the window. She could see the trees waving and a green basket turning like a wheel in the wind. "I saw him again," Maya said, her heart pounding.

"Who?"

"Hackett, the one who interviewed me, about the sonnoluminescence project in the restaurant," Maya said.

"Where?" Ashman asked.

Maya was nervous, and frightened. She lit a cigarette, still looking out the window at the green basket that was turning like a wheel. "Today at the parade. Across the street when you went for the balloon. You were with him."

Ashman didn't like it. What was the Major doing interviewing Maya? What did he want with such a piddling matter as her college research? Why didn't the Major tell him? he asked himself.

Maya went on, "I don't like this. What's going on? You and him?" she asked, although she knew he would never tell her.

"Stupid business," Ashman told her. "They always think they're smarter than everybody else. It's always their undoing, those stupid government contracting officers." Ashman sat down on the couch. "Shall I kill him for you?" he asked her.

She surprised him, "Yes. I want none of them here. I want none of them in our lives. I just want us." She put her head on Ashman's shoulder and he ran his fingers through her hair.

When Maya fell asleep that night in their double bed, he left.

Business

It was a long day for Emil Dakkas. His flight had been delayed and the next one was canceled. He was glad to be home, even though Sophie and their little girl were sleeping by the time he came in. When Dakkas opened the front door, his big dog burst outside. Emil grabbed him by his collar. They walked around the yard together, setting off the motion detector lights as they did.

Dakkas went back inside and looked in on his wife and daughter. Then he checked the rest of the house and went into the kitchen to eat. There were two cold lamb chops in the refrigerator and Emil spread them with seeded mustard and sliced a tomato. He sat down to eat while he read the paper. The dog sat at his right hand waiting for a piece of meat.

Emil started with the sports section as he always did. Football season was at its height and basketball was just beginning, but he preferred baseball, having played two years in college. Next year, the family would go to Florida to see a spring training game and the manatees, which were a cause that Sophie had taken up. There was an article in the paper about another series of unexplained manatee deaths. He decided to read it after the sports page and then circle it for Sophie.

When Dakkas was done with the sports page, he turned to the entertainment section to check on the movies and television. "The closer you get to the front page," he had told Sophie "the closer you are getting to the funny pages." There was a fight on at 10:00. Red James was fighting for the World Boxing Union title, whatever that was. Dakkas decided that he'd skip it. It was all a lot of crap, he thought, the WBA, WBC, WBO, WBF, WBU, IBF, IBC, alphabet crap. He looked for a late-night movie.

Dakkas needed to be as tired as he could before he lay down. He had begun waking up at 4:10 a.m. again every morning, feeling there was something imperative to do, but not being sure what that was. Emil finished the dishes, wiped off the counter and went up to bed.

While he was checking on Sonny, Emil heard a noise downstairs. He thought it was likely the Dane nosing in the sink, but he went down the back stairway, racking a Glaser round into the chamber of his weapon.

There was a coffee filter and grounds on the floor and the big dog was lying in the corner of the kitchen, looking guilty. Even so, Dakkas went through the rest of the house. They had a cellular back-up for their alarm and he checked that and the phone.

Everything was secure. He looked in on Sonny again. As he walked up the hall to his bedroom, he could hear Sophie sleep-breathing loudly and he had to nudge her twice to make room for him. He lay down, hoping he would sleep through until just after six when the Dane would come in to wake him up, that he would not awaken four o'clock. Then he tried not to think of waking up because he did not want that thought in his head at all.

Emil Dakkas awoke at 4:10. It was still dark. His mind was racing that there was something he had to do. He did not know what it was. Dakkas checked the house and the yard; then did some shadowboxing to drain off some of the agitation. It was still dark, so he left the outside lights on and the one in the kitchen.

Emil went upstairs and pulled the covers around his daughter and then went back to lie down next to Sophie, who was half awake. She rubbed his hand. "I love you, honey," she said and she fell back to sleep.

He lay there awake for almost an hour. The clock said 5:30. Dakkas could smell dog shit in the hall. He got up and saw that there was a stinking pile near the linen closet.

"Fuck!" Emil said out loud. He took a piece of cardboard and a plastic bag from the shirt he was going to wear that morning. He cleaned up the mess and went downstairs. The dog was by the back door.

As he went to put the bag in the trash, the dog ran outside and stood up on the little hill across from the garage. Emil went to get the dog, taking his gun with him. He was not at all happy to be outside in the dark carrying his weapon and a bag of dog shit.

The motion lights around the corner of the house went on as Dakkas started back in. He wiped the safety off his Sig Sauer .45. Then he saw it was the Great Dane, who had run back up the little hill and was barking at the Japanese maple tree. The huge dog was barking and turning in half circles around the tree. When the dog came down the hill to go inside, Dakkas was sure it was a possum rather than a prowler.

Emil put the dog in his pen and locked up the house. But as he walked past the window, he thought he saw a man behind the tree. Dakkas grabbed his shotgun from the locked broom closet and went out the side door, arming the alarm. He ran straight at the tree, but from an angle behind it.

There was no one there. Dakkas waited downstairs for another hour before he went up to shower and start the day.

* * *

Emil Dakkas and Billy Orr met for breakfast at the Dreamline Diner. They did that every Monday morning when they could. The diner used to be long and silver, "like the Lone Ranger's silver bullet" they said, but now it was a blue box with high blue seats.

"You don't look so good," Dakkas told Orr. "You look like shit."

"That good, pardner?" Billy answered.

Orr had not slept well the last two nights and his eyes were puffy. He wondered whether Emil had seen him in his yard last night, although he knew he couldn't. Sometimes Orr thought he should tell him, or that he knew that he came there sometimes in the dark when he couldn't sleep.

"You all right, brother?" Dakkas asked.

"Old stuff," he answered, rubbing his left hand with his right. He didn't like to talk about the bad things from the war. Neither did anyone else who had been there unless they were drunk or crazy, but he didn't want Dakkas to think it was something else either.

Billy remembered a time they had talked about it. It was at his bachelor party. There was another guy there, a gunnery sergeant, named Costello, who worked for the school district and who walked bad because of two artificial knees. The three of them had gotten drunk together off to the side.

The gunnery sergeant had been at the same hospital he was, the Naval Hospital in Memphis, but at a different time. Everyone had been to the one on Guam.

The sergeant was drunk at the bachelor party, and laughing about this mama-san doing a hundred yard dash across a paddy with her pants around her ankles, and then he started saying, "We was all hacked-up and helpless. You couldn't go nowhere. I knew no one was safe." He said that last part two or three times.

It was in the Mustang Room and the three of them were kind of leaning on each other to stand up, because they were drunk and because of the sergeant's knees.

"How 'bout, it gents?" said the assistant manager, who was trying to close up the place.

"I'll move when I'm ready," said Costello. He tried to push Dakkas and Billy Orr away. "I stand alone," he said and he started to cry. "We was all hacked-up and helpless," he kept saying over and over.

Their breakfast came. Orr put ketchup on his eggs like he always did, but that morning he saw the ketchup ribbon run like a bloody road. He had the look in his eyes that he had searched everywhere for a sign that would give him a way to save himself and found none.

"I'll be right back," Billy said as he got up. He went to the men's room and splashed cold water on his round face and took a Xantax. He tried to pee, but couldn't. The drug kicked in, or the idea that it did, and when he came out he was okay. Emil had waited for him to eat.

"Sorry," Orr said when he came back.

"For what?"

"For remembering the day I found out I wasn't charmed."

"I heard that," Dakkas said. He called for the waiter and some more hot water for his tea.

Dakkas and Orr ate bacon and eggs and talked about their assignments. They could do that because they placed their brotherhood over everything else. A brotherhood three times over, from the war, by marriage, and from their present work for Uncle Sam.

"Fallon? You know him?" Dakkas asked.

"Charlie Fallon. He's dead."

"No another Fallon. Also goes by the name Feenane."

"Bad guy?" Orr asked him.

"Spook."

"Ours?"

"Who knows that anymore," Dakkas answered.

"You got that right."

"You alright, partner?" Dakkas asked.

"I'll be fine now that I'm up and moving," Billy answered as he paid the check.

"I heard that," Dakkas told him.

Loose Ends

Ray Sabatino was mean and cunning and wanted revenge. "Cut off his balls," is what he meant to do to Ashman. And Ashman's girlfriend, he meant to burn her up.

He wouldn't do that himself. It took a special expertise, and he had contracted for it before. Once he stayed so he could hear and see, and much to his surprise, smell, the burning-up of a certain rat, John-John "Rabbits" Molinari, burn up in his apartment. "Rabbits" weighed over three hundred pounds, so it took a long time. It was odd, Sabatino thought, that with all the screaming, it smelled like a barbecue. Ray Sabatino hoped Ashman could smell his ownself and his girl burning up. He smiled when he thought of that.

Sabatino drove to Tenafly, New Jersey to pick up Nicky Primavera to do the job. It was the first time he had used him. The other torch he had used got careless and went up in an insurance job in a furniture warehouse in Queens. Sabatino was not happy when they met because he had been stuck in the Holland Tunnel for an hour. One of the tunnel cops couldn't stand life in the little booth any more and ran onto the road and then couldn't move.

Nicky, the torch, shocked Sabatino when they met because he was so tall. Ray thought he'd have trouble fitting in the car.

"Three grand, plus transportation," the torch told him. "I coulda charged you five, six grand on account of the job is where it is, but you get off as a professional courtesy, provided you get approval. Plus I'm givin' you another yard off on account of the ride," Nicky said. He had lost his driver's license for thirty days due to a drinking and driving conviction. "And it's good to have new clientele," he added as Sabatino started up his maroon Cadillac.

It surprised Emil Dakkas that Ray Sabatino had picked up somebody so openly. From the intel he had been provided, it was more than likely just another facet of his "I don't give a shit. I know it all" attitude. Dakkas didn't know who the guy was. He would improvise, but stay within his assignment.

Major Coates had put him on Sabatino that morning. "You were there when Frankie Cigars got his. That's a bad thing. It complicates. It makes loose ends. We'll turn it into a mob war by taking this Sabatino out up close with a .22. I want an execution, not a field operation. And I want it soon."

Dakkas stayed two or three cars in back of Ray Sabatino's Cadillac as they came down the Parkway. He had been following him since before he picked up Nicky Primavera in North Jersey. Twice he pulled ahead so if anything, it looked like the Caddy was following him.

Sabatino got on the New Jersey Turnpike going south, which told Dakkas they were either going to get off at Trenton or Philly, or they were going to Atlantic City. Dakkas ruled that out because they could have taken the Parkway all the way down.

Sabatino pulled into the next rest stop because Nicky's farts were smelling up the car. "I gotta remember not to eat them nuts," he said apologetically.

Dakkas followed them into the reststop and parked behind a tractor trailer so he could watch the car and the restaurant. He thought that if it was darker out or if the parking lot was not filled, that he could take Sabatino there, but Dakkas was patient.

He went back onto the Turnpike and pushed it at seventy miles per hour. He pulled over to the right and waited for Sabatino. When they drove by, Dakkas followed and stayed close.

It was dark when both cars went over the Walt Whitman Bridge into South Philadelphia. Sabatino's outdated information told him Maya Charcot was staying there. He knew he had to meet with Carlo, "Jimmy Two Plates," Gigante, who, though he was old and half blind, had to be given his respect. This was because the house where Maya was staying was in his neighborhood, and because Sabatino was coming in from out of town to do a job and bringing in Nicky Primavera from North Jersey.

Ray Sabatino left Nicky in the car while he went into the Columbus Social Club for his meeting with Jimmy Two Plates, who he would call "Don Carlo" or "Mr. Gigante" out of respect.

"You got a nice family," Carlo said. "My niece is god-mother to your wife's sister."

"Thank you," Ray answered. He waited until it was polite to talk about business. Johnnie Gigante, Carlo's nephew, brought over red wine which Sabatino sipped before he started."I've come out of respect..."

"That's nice. You got a nice family," Don Carlo told him.

"It's business," Sabatino began again.

"Bizz-i-ness," answered Jimmy Two Plates. He was wearing his hat inside, but took it off to eat.

Dakkas came in and shot them both. The old man was facing him, so he took him first. Completing his smooth arc, he shot Ray Sabatino in the eye, whose head turned slightly at the sound of the first shot. Dakkas shot him again behind the ear as was fitting the type of job it was supposed to be. The shots went, "Crack, crack, crack."

It took less than ten seconds for Dakkas to enter the room, take his targets, squeeze off the three rounds and leave. By the time Johnnie Gigante came out from the kitchen to serve the bowl of pasta and peas, Dakkas had thrown a handful of pennies on the two dead men and walked back outside.

When Dakkas came out from doing his job he saw Sabatino's passenger running up the street and turning the corner. The torch had asked Ray to leave his keys in the Caddy so he could listen to the radio, but Ray wouldn't. "Christ, you're a drunk driver," Ray had told him. The torch was out and moving at the sound of the three shots.

Emil Dakkas thought of taking-out the running man, but he

knew not to freestyle and if it was supposed to look like a mob hit, the tall guy could be described as the hit man. Dakkas followed him in killing range until they got to the bus station where Primavera took a bus back to New Jersey.

Emil drove back over the bridge, staying in the far right lane. He knew that somebody crossing the center line was as much a threat to him as doing the job itself.

The trip back was direct and uneventful. He called Major Coates as he had been directed. "Fine," he told the Major.

"That's fine," the Major answered.

They would meet face to face within the next twenty-four hours when he had to present his report. In the meantime he would return to his assignment on Fallon.

After Coates got his call from Dakkas, he left for dinner at the Republic, driving the long route and parking in his usual lot. John, the doorman, was waiting for him when he came in. "Good afternoon, Major. Dinner today, sir?" he asked.

"I thought I'd have a shave first, John," the Major told him. He went down the stairs to the lower level where the pool and barber shop were. He could smell the chlorine from the pool which he had written to the House Committee about on two occasions.

The barber shop was closed. As he was going back up the stairs, the bartender came down. "He's closed, Your Honor," the bartender said. "Prostrate cancer. Pity, ain't it? That's the way it is, I guess. He can't go at all, and me going to the Gents every half hour."

The Major ordered a Boodles in the dining room. As he was

lighting his cigar, a waiter came over. He was sweating. "I'm sorry, sir," he told the Major. "Management requests no cigar smoking in the dining room," he said, gesturing to the new sign discretely lettered, but prominently placed. The sign read: "At the suggestion of the House Committee, the Board of Governors has now enacted a prohibition against pipe or cigar smoking in the dining room."

"Who is the dining manager this evening?" The Major asked. "Who is in the office?"

"I don't know, sir. I will 'ask' for you," the waiter said.

The Major winced, at the language.

"Excuse me?" the waiter asked.

"Never mind." Major Coates told him. "Bring me my usual. If you don't know what it is, find out."

When the waiter came back with a gin and tonic, the Major tasted his drink and lit his cigar. Somewhat later than usual, his salad arrived and then almost immediately afterwards, the lamb chops which he had not ordered.

"Why don't you 'aks' who ordered the lamb," Major Coates told the waiter. "The steak, wherever it is, is mine."

While the Major ate his salad and finished his drink, the evening manager came in and explained the "no-cigar" policy, averting his gaze from the Ashton which the Major had rested on his plate. "We are making arrangements for dining in the Sitting Room, Major," he said. "In the meantime, enjoy your meal."

When the steak arrived, the Major did enjoy it and afterwards had his car brought around. "Good evening, Major," the doorman told him as he left. "I hope your evening was a pleasant one."

"All in all, John. All in all," the Major answered. He was happy that another loose end had been removed. Ray Sabatino could have led to Franca to Doyle to Frankie Cigars to him. Emil Dakkas had made it nice and neat for him.

Symmetry

Major Coates kept the temperature in his house at sixty degrees. The only rug was to cover a pressure sensor for the burglar alarm. The furniture was plain and sparse, an eerie juxtaposition to the large room of computers upstairs. He lived alone except for a pair of German shepherds, his "two ladies," he called them.

It was five o'clock in the morning when the dogs woke the Major by climbing on his bed. As he had been getting up that early since as long as he could remember, he went downstairs. Coates let his dogs out, one from the front door and one from the back.

When they started barking, he went to the windows to check. He could see them running along the fence line that went up to the road. The Major called them in, standing behind the steel-lined front door with his Colt Commander in his hand. The dogs returned and he sent them back out again in thirty seconds.

Only when "his ladies" began to play, was the Major confident that there were no intruders on the grounds.

There was a large living room off of the hall which served as the Major's gymnasium. He put a cassette in the VCR and rode his ski machine.

After a breakfast of fruit and two poached eggs, Coates went upstairs to work. The older dog remained in front of the back door, the younger one went upstairs with him. The Major placed his right hand on the door of his computer room and his face against the retinal screen. When the scans identified him, the door lock clicked open and he went inside. He slid his chair over to the center of the four monitors which surrounded him.

On one of the screens he brought up a diagram of what he called his "Projects and Players." The Major reviewed the present state of circumstances. He could see that Dakkas had killed Knoddles, who had killed Fulliard Stevens. Stevens had worked with Maya Charcot, who was Ashman's girlfriend. Frankie Cigars put Ashman in the Elms. Ashman had killed him. Dakkas had taken-out Ray Sabatino to cover that. The Major had put Orr on Ashman. Dakkas was Orr's brother-in-law. The Major had put Ashman on him. Orr, Dakkas, and Ashman were after Fallon. He loved the symmetry of it.

Major Coates put his evaluation of the sonnoluminescence project on the screen to his left. He examined and reexamined all the perspectives: Dr. Charcot, Switt, Greenglass, Stevens, the Israelis, Fallon, and General Kendall. He reviewed each new development and piece of intelligence on the downing of Flight 800.

Fortunately, as General Kendall had told him, all the investigations into the cause of the downing of Flight 800 were fruit-less and there was no mention in any documents of the use of domestic 747's for intelligence purposes or of the Israelis. It relieved the Major that any error he may have made on the sound-to-light project appeared to be incidental. This made Fallon's approach all the more curious and therefore, all the more of concern.

Coates went to his computer system for data on his Non Lethal Weapons Projects and directed this to the third screen. He wondered if perhaps Fallon might be involved in one of them. He could find nothing of interest.

On the fourth sceen were the people who the Major was in personal contact with, including his ex-wife, who lived in Scarsdale, the General, and Isabella Enchant. The Major also used that fourth screen to examine old relationships. This included people he had known in Vietnam, but not Ashman who was tangential then.

Kyle Lee Coates sat in the center of the room and studied each of the screens, individually, and then with another. He believed all of it, and trusted none of it.. He knew that in the world of espionage that is was just as likely that things were not what they did not appear to be as that they were not what they appeared to be.

The Major felt that his plans and systems were well thought-out and functioning effectively, except as far as Fallon was con-cerned. If Fallon had not come to see him about the sound to light project and Flight 800, what was his angle, his purpose? He could be a probe from an unseen enemy or part of a domes-tic political cabal. That gave him a gnawing feeling that there was something going on that he knew nothing about and that somehow, would point directly at him.

He went outside to walk his dogs. The dogs ran with him and around in circles. The younger shepherd came and licked the Major's hand. Coates felt her teeth beneath the kiss. He returned to his computers and reviewed the information on Isabella Enchant.

Isabella's mother's name was Francesca O'Barra. Her father's name was William Wagner. They divorced when she was six. The name "Enchant" was something Isabella had made up. Her health was good, except for her allergies. The Major couldn't understand why she kept a cat. She had two gyno procedures which likely were abortions. Lots of dental work including a half dozen caps, probably from her bruxism, he thought. He could hear her grinding her teeth in her sleep. No criminal record except some early "disturbing the peace" things from her college politics. Isabella belonged to the NRA; she said it excited her. She had a bad driving record which included three illegal left turns at the same corner on the same day.

Her financial history showed one hundred eighty thousand dollars in the Bank of Boston, which traced back to a trust fund and further back to the proceeds from the father's estate. He was killed by a tractor trailer carrying electrical parts.

Isabella had two long periods of employment at the Kamm School where she taught French and German, and from which she collected a biweekly compensation check for a fractured coccyx resulting from a fall. Her insurance carrier had paid a property theft claim; her bag and camera were stolen from her car in Soho. The carrier dropped her after the left-turn tickets. Her last vehicle was a 1977 Pacer registered to her in Seattle, Washington.

The data the Major had already gathered and his own observations about her fit the same profile of the eccentric, self-possessed, artist-type. It also was consistent with the recent fact that Isabella had just packed up and moved away. She had done that several times in the past. He knew however, that thorough intelligence gathering required a final, detailed examination of her apartment.

As Major Coates drove to Isabella's, he realized that of all the people he had been interacting with, he had acted with the least caution with her. He could see police lights as he came around her corner. There were also two fire engines in front of her brownstone building and two police cruisers, one up on the sidewalk.

He parked as close as he could get to the scene and walked halfway down the block. One of the uniforms walked up to him, "No, admission," the uniform said.

"Thank you, patrolman," the Major answered. "Tell whoever is in charge that I'm to go through. I'll wait here for him."

"No press," the patrolman added.

"Thank you. Please convey my message, <u>now</u>."

The patrolman looked at him hard, but did as Major Coates asked. One of the detectives came over and examined the Major's I.D. which included a directive: "Do not detain. Major Kyle Lee Coates is acting on the direct orders of the President of the United States."

"No shit," the detective said.

The sector car pulled up and the lieutenant got out. He was a fat man with a bald head. "What's the military want with this?" the lieutenant asked Major Coates.

"That's on a need to know basis, Lieutenant," the Major told him. "What happened here?"

"Well, I need-to-know, and you need to know this is my case. My name is Lumen, if you need to write it down."

The Major took out his cell phone. "Shall I call your chief at home? How is Mike these days? Or the Agent in Charge at the Bureau? I need to know what your crime scene is about."

Lieutenant Lumen relented. If the Major called his boss there'd be hell to pay, he thought, and the F.B.I. was a pain in the ass. "They come in, two of them, to steal this guys birds, parrots," he told the Major. "Big ones, I'm told they're worth thousands. Then they start flapping their wings and squawking and screaming and one of the perps runs out and the other one shoots one of the birds, and the other big parrots got him scared to death. He's in there beggin' to get out. It's like, a fucking Tarzan movie."

Lumen and the Major walked over to Isabella's building, stepping over the fire hoses on the sidewalk. They went into the vestibule, following one of the detectives who cracked the door. There were big birds flying all around, squawking and screaming and they could see the shadow of someone hiding behind a chair.

"We told the perp behind the chair to stop screaming or they'd tear him up," the detective said. "One of the firemen nearly got his hand bit off.

"Hyacinths," the Major told them.

"What?" Lieutenant Lumen asked.

"Hyacinth Macaws. They're the birds. Worth about twenty grand apiece. Anything doing in the apartment upstairs?"

"She called the fire department," the detective answered, but she won't come out."

"I'll extract her," the Major answered, "without disturbing your scene."

He went upstairs. The apartment was still empty. Isabella was sitting on a ladder in the back room, crying. She was wearing painter's clothes with the pants cuffs rolled up and the bill of the cap sideways. She looked up as he came in and walked across the dropcloths to her.

"You all right?" he asked, putting his hand on her leg.

"Lots of b's and c's," she answered.

He looked at her.

"Musical notes," she said, pointing to the mascara that had run onto her cheek. "I cried from the opera of the birds' screaming. I pulled the firebox."

"There was a robbery downstairs. Are you all right?" the Major asked.

"I'm painting it all lavender. It's my favorite color," she said, gesturing to the wall behind her. "I need a bath. So does Pinky Tony. He's so very allergic, so very yin."

"Where is your cat?" the Major asked her.

"He's taking a bath at the groomer."

"Grab some things."

Isabella brought out a big leather bag and some clothes, a book, and her pillow. "Can I stay at your place for a while," she asked. She went into the bathroom, dragging the bag behind and filled it with her make-up and personal things and then some cheese she recently bought. "I don't have any wine," Isabella told him as they left.

The Major and Isabella drove on for awhile. He stopped for Chinese food at the Ming Palace. The restaurant was owned by a former Thai Air Force major, who seemed to remember the Major, although they had not met before. As they continued on to his home, Isabella ate the chicken and cashews with her fingers. "El Topo to my rescue again," she said.

"Who?" he asked

"He was a Zen cowboy."

"I'm not that."

"I think you are that," she said. Isabella put her hand on his leg and then her head on his shoulder, poking him with the painter's hat. She turned the hat around so the bill was in the back. Her face looked rounder and older.

The Major opened the window a bit and lit a Carrington, inhaling the first bit of smoke. Isabella asked for a cigar and he gave her one.

"Do you have one of those thingamabobs?" she asked.

"A what?"

"One of those nipper things," Isabella told him. She had her head on his shoulder and was eating the Chinese food from the paper container and fiddling with the cigar. Isabella started to bite the end off her cigar, but he stopped her.

"I'll do it," he told her. "If you don't do it right, either you don't get the right draw or you unravel it all." He snipped the end off of her cigar and lit it, turning it and drawing on the flame which jumped with his breath. He handed it to her. She inhaled and coughed.

"Just taste it," he said.

Isabella puffed on the cigar a bit and then fell asleep. She woke when the Major stopped for gas and stayed awake until they were nearly home.

"Shall I carry you?" he asked her when he pulled up to his home.

"I weigh a ton," she answered. "I always eat when I redecorate."

Major Coates disarmed the alarm and put the dogs in "sit and stay." They watched Isabella carefully as she took off her painter's cap. "Do you like it?" she asked the Major.

He was surprised at her blonde hair.

"I look like Doris Day," Isabella said.

"I think that's right," he told her.

"You'll like it better when it grows in. I'll look like someone else." Isabella sat down on the edge of the sofa. "I'll look like early Deborah Harry, but right now I feel like Dirty Harry. I'm going to take a shower now. Then later, we can take a bath."

He let the dogs out as Isabella went into the bathroom and ran the shower. The steam was coming up under the door. The Major looked through her big bag. There was nothing there that surprised him: her clothes, the food, three packs of gum, a hair brush, a travel container for tampons, her diaphragm case, two starter sizes of perfume, a beeper that did not work, a bottle of grape seed extract, three Xanax .25's, lots of make-up, and an address book.

He studied that. The only names he recognized were her two ex-husbands and his. Isabella had her own phone numbers in the book, the present one and the one before it. There were two names in Virginia: "Uncle Albert" and "Sandi Cimino," and three from Seattle. When the bathroom door started to open, the Major put the address book away. Isabella's skin was bright pink from the hot shower and she opened the terry cloth robe to show him.

"I need you," Isabella said.

"Let me lock up first," he told her, even though he had a strong erection.

The Major brought his dogs back in. He locked the front door and checked the back and armed the alarms. Isabella was already in the bedroom waiting for him, singing to herself. When the Major came in to the bedroom, she stepped out from behind the door and shot him twice in the back of the neck with the compact .38 she had taken into the bathroom. The Major dropped like a rock, his throat blown out.

Isabella stopped the spreading blood with a towel and quickly took off his clothes, which she put on to aid in her getaway. She put her underwear on Major Coates and applied a quick course of makeup to his draining face.

After taking the Major's wallet and jewelry, she opened the bedroom door, standing behind it as the dogs rushed in. She killed them both and walked down the stairs and out the front door.

Confrontation

Ashman checked the mechanism of his Browning Hi-Power hand gun and five shot AMT back-up and slipped in his boot knife. He put the canister of pepper fog in his jacket and jumped up and down to see if anything made noise. The loc-pic on his key ring jingled, so he wrapped small tape strips around it.

He picked up his large canvas bag containing the C4, which he had removed from Maya's house, and carried out to his vehicle. The rest of his belongings were already in the four-wheel drive he had secured for the trip. He would not be coming back.

If he was in combat, if he was in the shit, Ashman knew to stand his post or engage the enemy, but that wasn't what was going on. Something, all of it, wasn't right at Maya's and he didn't know what that was. It all felt wrong like he had taken a wrong turn, like things had been moved.

Whenever that happened, he knew to leave. Ashman knew that was how he managed to stay alive and also, he knew, to be a fifty year old man with no family and no home.

Ashman checked his vehicle, the filament tape on the doors, trunk, and hood. He looked behind the wheels and at the under-carriage. He unlocked the car doors with the remote across the street. The safeguards were not foolproof, but they were a line of defense except against those who would get to him no matter what he did.

They were the ones he had to get. The ones who put him in the hospital, the ones who killed Doyle. They would come back and kill him in his sleep. He meant to get them first.

He had to be at work Tuesday morning, which gave him time to get a new place to live and to make a trip to the Elms. Ashman didn't leave unfinished business, particularly when it could kill him.

As he drove away, he thought how Maya's backyard looked like Franca's and then about , how Major Coates had put him on Fallon. The Major told him that Dakkas was also sent after Fallon and that he should follow Dakkas. Ashman knew that meant, just as likely as not, that Dakkas would be following him. He also considered that Fallon, or the Major himself, could be a fake or, even what they called a "fake fake."

Ashman drove for twenty minutes, staying in the right lane, two car lengths behind a Mercedes in front of him. He took the next exit.

There was a fast-food restaurant at the foot of the ramp. He pulled in and ordered drive-thru. It wasn't sundown yet and since he wanted to work in the dark, he followed the road to the left to the Cinema Nine Theater and waited there for the night to come down.

When the movie let out, the roads were crowded and it had started to rain. His trip to the Elms took longer than he expected, but Ashman always gave himself extra time. Even at Maya's, the clocks were twelve minutes ahead. He arrived slightly before the shifts were changing.

Ashman came in from the parking lot, passing between the parked cars. Two men, one short with a beard and one taller and leaning on a cane, were standing with a red haired, roundish woman in the back doorway of the Administration Building. They were talking and smoking cigarettes.

He went around to the delivery entrance and through the kitchen carrying his flashlight in his teeth. An old Irish setter slept in the corner of the kitchen. It raised its head, but the flashlight bothered the dog's eyes and it went back to sleep.

The halls were empty so that his trip to the medical records room was quick and easy. The door to that office was locked, but he picked the lock and went in. There were files stacked everywhere, in alphabetical order, but in parts. Ashman couldn't find his own file anywhere or any that looked like his. He went to the computer room three doors down.

The computer room was in similar disarray. He could hear someone coming down the hall. The footsteps sounded like a woman's. When she came to the door of the computer room, Ashman stepped into the shadows. It was the red headed woman who had been outside smoking. Ashman waited until she was at her desk, processing the stack of manila files.

"What's your name?" he asked from the shadows.

She was startled but thought she recognized the voice as a patient's. "You should be in your room," she said.

"No," said Ashman. He came out of the shadows, wearing all black with his face blacked-out. He turned off the lights and was behind her before she could cry out.

Ashman put his hand on her shoulder to frighten and to comfort her. "This has nothing to do with you. You haven't seen me so I don't have to kill you. I won't rape you. I won't hurt you. You can smoke if you want."

"What?" she said.

"You can smoke. What is your name?" Ashman asked her calmly.

"Rhonda Hummel," she told him.

"Rhonda, this is not your business. It has nothing to do with you. Do what I tell you and you'll be fine. You can smoke if you want to." He shined the bright flashlight on her handbag.

She took a cigarette from the packing her handbag and lit up. "I'm okay," she said, exhaling the smoke she had double inhaled.

"Access me all the patients on the second floor between November 1st and November 15th of this year," he told her. She started to look back at him, but stopped when he shone the flashlight onto her computer. She did as he asked.

Ashman found two patients who might be who he was looking for, Robert Chitwood and Hobart Hoak. "Good job," he told her. "Good girl. Let me see their papers."

The records scrolled up and Ashman studied them. There were only the intake diagnosis and the manner of admission. Both patients were diagnosed as having hysterical paralysis. They were both admitted on Dr. Misheloff's service.

"Does Misheloff smoke cigars?"

"What?" she said. She turned towards him, but he had moved across the room. She lit another cigarette.

"Does Misheloff smoke cigars?" Ashman repeated.

"Oh, yes," she answered.

"Does anyone else who has access to those patients?"

"Does anyone else what?"

"Smoke cigars?"

"Not that I know of," she answered. His flashlight was shining at her again and she had to shield her eyes.

"We're going to Misheloff's office. I'll be right behind you. You won't see me. When you get there, go directly to his desk and sit there with your hands in front of you. If his door is locked, I'll open it. I'll leave as soon we're done there." He motioned her up. "You're doing fine, Rhonda. I'll be out of here soon," he paused. "You're very nice."

She got up and went to the door. Ashman was nowhere in sight. "You can't smoke in the hall," she said over to the shadows.

Dr. Misheloff's office was four offices down the hall. The door was locked when she got there and she turned around to show that. Ashman was on her quick, passing his right arm under hers to pick the lock, spinning her back toward the door so she couldn't see him. She smelled of stale cigarettes and had a cluster of skin tags on her neck, but she was built well and Ashman thought she backed in against him at the door.

When the door was open, Ashman pointed to on the seat. "Chitwood and Hoak," he told her.

"I'll look," she answered.

Dr. Misheloff kept no files, only orange patient cards in a large oak filing cabinet behind his big desk. The drawers that were his were marked "M-1." The others were either for the other doctors or were empty.

The only entries on the orange cards for Hoak and Chitwood were the diagnoses: "Hysterical Paralysis," their date of admission and discharge, and that they were both private pay patients. The referring physicians were physicians' groups, Medtrex and PsychMed Associates. The names meant nothing to Ashman.

"Who are PsychMed and Medtrex?" Ashman asked. Rhonda didn't know anything more than that from time to time they sent patients to Dr. Misheloff.

"I'm going now," Ashman told her. "You've done fine." He could hear her breathing in the dark. "The cleaning man," he asked her. "He must be a patient here, Rhonda, singing all the time. Where is he?"

"He'll be over in B Building. He has to be there by eight and then they lock it," she answered.

"You're very nice," Ashman told her. He turned off his light and lightly touched her hand. "Should I...?"

"Oh," she said, nervous and anxious. She went out and up the hall to her office, looking over her shoulder. He was not there.

Ashman saw the cleaning man coming down the hall, talking to himself. He stepped out of the shadows alongside of him. "Wait," he told the cleaning man.

"Wait, wait," Nash answered as he kept going. "Wait, wait." Ashman grabbed his arm to stop him.

"No, no," said Nash, his eyes as big as they could get. "No, No, No, No." And then he started to cry, rubbing his face like a child.

"What's going on?" asked Dr. Misheloff, who had come up the hall. Ashman stepped back in the shadows and drew his blade. He could smell the cigar odor he had smelled when he was strapped down and helpless. The doctor was a little man in a dark suit. He wore rimless glasses and a polka dot bow tie. He walked with his hands in his pockets.

"I'm here, Delbert," Dr. Misheloff told Nash. "Look at me, I'm here."

"Here, here, here, here," Nash said, four times as he did everything when he was agitated. He looked at the rug he was standing on. It had designs like flying fish and golden stars floating in the sea. Nash felt the flying fish and the golden stars go all the way to the sky and back down around him and his yellow boots. He fell down.

Ashman came out of the shadows and grabbed Dr. Misheloff by the throat, pulling him into the darkness. "We're going to have a little talk, little man," he told the doctor. "Just you and me."

Misheloff gagged.

"We're going to your office," Ashman told him.

"Now?" the doctor stammered.

Ashman loosened his grip on the doctor's trachea. "Wouldn't you rather see me in the daytime?" Misheloff asked.

"I like the dark. Come with me now or I'll slit your throat."

"Isn't this a bit over-dramatic?" Misheloff said. He walked slowly, trying to stall for someone to come by or to find a way to defuse his attacker. "You're being unreasonable and so mysterious."

Ashman pushed the doctor into the shadows, putting the point of his blade in the hollow of his throat. "We're all unreasonable and covert, Cigarman. Last chance. Your office or your life. I'll take either."

"That's fine. That's fine," the psychiatrist said. "I'm happy to go with you." Ashman took him quickly down the hall to his office. "What do you want to talk about?" he asked Ashman. He began to remove his right hand from his pocket to open his office door.

"Freeze!" Ashman said firmly. "You put your hands in your pockets, you leave them there." He reached around the doctor and punched in the numbers that he had seen the woman do a few minutes before.

"Ah," Misheloff said as they went inside his office, "A patient? A disgruntled employee?" he asked. He reached for the light switch, but Ashman intercepted his hand with his knife.

"I'm your nightmare."

"We all have those from time to time," the psychiatrist said. He walked over to his desk.

Ashman waved him off, "I'll sit there. For the next twenty minutes or so, I'm the shrink. If you lie to me, I'm going to cut out part of your brain. I will like that. Here's the way it's going to work. I'm going to ask you questions and you're going to answer me. If you fuck with me, I'm going to hurt you permanently so you can't talk or see. Then I'm going to hurt your family. I'm going to cut them up. If you try and run, I'll shoot you down like a dog. I'll sever your spine and then I'll cut your eyes out." He produced his gun with the other hand.

"You <u>are</u> angry at me," the doctor said.

Ashman smiled a bit, and went on, "I have a second rule. If you try to manipulate me, I'm going to cut your penis off and put it in your shirt pocket. Please understand, I mean everything I say quite literally. And I will do what I say. I have done it before, more than once. You're only a picture in a magazine to me, a talking cut-out. I won't feel a thing when I hurt you. Understand?"

"Understood," Dr. Misheloff answered.

"Who is PsychoMed Associates? Who owns it?" Ashman asked him.

"You were a patient of theirs here?"

Ashman slowly raised his gun and cocked the hammer. "You forgot what I told you, Doctor. I'm not going to remind you again."

"I'm sorry," Misheloff said. "Harold Edel owns it. You know, 'Dr. Divorce' on television. But he's not here."

Ashman lowered his gun. "Anybody else run it? Own a piece?" He leaned over from his side of the desk with his other hand and cut a button off the doctor's jacket with his blade. "You?" he asked.

"I don't know who. Not me."

"Medtrex? Is that you?"

"No."

"That's a lie, Doc." Ashman cut off a second button and then cut a slice in Misheloff's shirt. "Next time I will cut off your nipple. That will bleed a lot." He moved forward. The doctor was trembling. "Medtrex?" Ashman asked again.

"Yes, Medtrex. I own part of it. With a managed care group from Los Angeles. I need to get up."

"No." Ashman told him.

"I have to go to the bathroom."

"No. Are they the only referral sources to your service?"

"There are dozens. Some are self-referred. I have to go to the bathroom."

"No," Ashman told him. "I want to know why I was a patient here. I want to know how. I want to know who. You can tell me. If you don't, I'm going to hurt you permanently so you can't talk or see. Then I'm going to cut off your penis and put it in your pocket. I'm going to kill your family. I'm going to cut them up."

"I understand. Let me go to the bathroom and then I'll help you. I've got a bad colon."

"No. Who is Chitwood?" Ashman asked.

"Chitwood?"

"Hoak?"

"Which one?" the doctor asked again.

"You tell me."

"There was a Chitwood who left the facility "AMA," Against Medical Advice, but that was last year," the doctor answered. "Hoak was here this year."

"Which ones escaped?"

"Look, I've got to go to the bathroom or I'm going to soil myself."

"Naughty little boy," Ashman said, "After we see their charts, I'll take you. Misheloff tried to keep his bowels from erupting by contracting his sphincter muscles even more.,

"I'll help you find what you are looking for," Dr. Misheloff told him.

"Of course you will."

"When I'm done, I'll get the records for you. Those two patients you mentioned had hysterical paralysis, if I recall. That is when the mind shuts the body down. From something too horrible for it to deal with." Misheloff felt an opportunity and tried to get at his captor. "Usually something catastrophic, like seeing your child get hit by a truck, or something horrible happening to you. It could be old, twenty-five years old. Opening up the war trunk you've kept locked at your mother's house, being locked up with the pictures you're afraid to see, and the old uniforms, the smell of camphor, and the smell of blood. You want to run and you can't. Or someone touching you that shouldn't."

Ashman laughed and hit him hard.

Dr. Misheloff shit himself. "Please," he said. "Let me wipe myself. The records are next door."

Ashman opened the door to go back into the hall, sending the doctor out first. Always whistle 'Dixie' when you're coming up from the tunnel. He half-expected to see a security guard or someone else in the hall, that Misheloff might have to talk them by. He did not expect the rifle shot that blew off the top of the doctor's head. The bullet hit Ashman in his bullet-proof vest right below his collar bone, knocking him down.

Ashman rolled down and away and back into the office and set up behind the large desk. For a moment there were no more shots.

The shooter fired three rounds in quick succession into the upper windows of the patients' wing. One of the shots hit a patient in the left hand as he ran by, gesturing wildly to close an imaginary deal.

Ashman ran down the hall to the heavy elevator that Nash had used to take him down into the tunnels. As the elevator descended, he remembered the smells and sounds of the hospital and the tunnel.

He heard Nash's voice reverberating in the catacombs as he

went down. Nash was telling stories to men sitting on a mattress.

"... And the little shiny fishes were swimming in the sun and the wave went by shining in the sun and the stars shined down and so did the waves of the water sea waves and of the sun sea waves. And all the swimming fishes were shining, shining. Home at last."

Ashman ran underground to the red ladder where he had taken the pair of yellow pants. He went up the ladder combat ready, banging the lid open with his left hand and coming up behind it in a shooting position. When he heard more shots, Ashman stopped, quickly, weighing whether he should go back down and find a way to come up behind the shooter. "Dixie," he said and came up.

A sniper was behind the big tree he had once watched from his hospital bed. The shooter saw him and snapped off two shots in his direction. Ashman was in Indian Country and his heart was pounding. He loved it.

He turned to the left and ran low through the parking lot after the shooter, who was heading towards the road. The shooter saw Ashman and swung up his H&K Special Op. It was a black night and although the sniper was dressed for it, his configuration and his body movement looked familiar.

Ashman looked for a kill shot, but there wasn't any because of the angle and the way the shooter hunkered down and zigzagged as he went through the other trees for the macadam road. Suddenly, for a moment there was a target as they both ran, changing angles. Ashman let off four shots. Two of them hit.

Police cars were coming, their sirens wailing in the distance. Ashman knew he was in the clear and had time. Even with the police vehicles coming, he could escape back down the tunnels. He went to check the shooter who was face down, his legs churning to turn or run. It was Billy Orr.

"Fuck!" Ashman said. It meant the whole thing was bad. He patted Orr down and took his sidearm, back-up piece, and blade. The body armor had stopped one of the shots, but one had gotten under the vest and Billy was bleeding heavily. "Fuck me or finish me," he said.

Ashman wanted answers. "I'm your EVAC, Orr." He fire-man-carried him to the ladder and took him down into the catacombs.

Billy was quiet until he got down the red ladder and Ashman had propped him up in the tunnel. He said "thanks" while he struggled to stanch the heavy blood with his wound kit. He was getting weak.

"Who?" Ashman applied Orr's pressure bandage to the wound. "Who?" he asked.

"You," Orr answered.

"Me?"

"For whacking the Major."

"Bullshit," Ashman told him. "On whose orders? What Agency? Who?" Ashman put his gun on Orr's heart.

"Sorry, friend. I may be dying, but..."

Ashman knew he was getting nothing. "There are docs upstairs and the law's on the way," he said. He carried Orr down the tunnel and laid him on a mattress. A flapping man ran by and showed his teeth. Every other one of them was black.

Billy Orr's eyes widened. "Metaphor," he called to the madman with the black and white teeth. "It's me, Smiley," he said as he passed out.

FireFight

Dakkas called home on his way back from killing Ray Sabatino. He got the answering machine.

"Hi, honey. It's me," he told himself. "Who's that man answering the phone? I'll be home for dinner. Going to stop for barbecue chicken."

It started to rain fast and heavy. The highway was crowded and the driving slow. He took a box of Chiclets from the compartment in the car door and shook some into his mouth. The trip took Dakkas almost an hour to get to Jack Kazanjian's deli rather than the usual twenty-five minutes.

"Hey, Emil," Kaz called from behind the counter. He wiped his hands on a red-striped towel tucked into his apron. "What can I get for you, my friend?" he asked.

"A couple of those barbecuties, Kaz."

Jack Kanzakian was round and dark and smelled like his cooking. He went over to the rotisserie. "They're small. They're small. I'll give you three of them. Same price."

"Thanks, my friend," Dakkas answered. "How's everything?"

"Good. Good." Kaz lowered his voice a bit as he speared the chickens off the turning spit. "That lump on Diana's breast turned out to be just a fibroid. God is good." He wrapped the three chickens in quilted tin foil, pouring some barbecue sauce in a container and pointing to the rotisserie.

"Yes. But don't tell my cardiologist."

Kaz spooned some of the chicken drippings into the sauce. "Mine neither," Kaz answered, running his finger in the spoon. "Rolls? Slaw?"

"No I'm good." Dakkas changed his mind and took a half dozen rolls, two of which he'd eat on the way home. He wished he had gotten an orange soda, but the ride was only fifteen minutes.

* * *

When Ashman came up from the tunnel at the Elms he went right at Emil Dakkas. It was a place to make an immediate start. Ashman needed answers and he knew that he would get them one way or another.

He thought about Dakkas as he drove in. He had seen his house before and the Great Dane. He would be in and out in fifteen minutes at the most, counting the trouble if there was going to be any. If it came to talk and Ashman didn't like what he heard, he'd kill Emil Dakkas without hesitation or mercy. If

he could, he'd get Dakkas outside of his house, as much to min-
imize any advantage as to spare the wife and kid.

Ashman was wearing blue coveralls with the name "Hal" in
an embroidered ellipse on the right breast pocket. In his pockets were a chalk line, wire cutters, and a union card. He had cut
the right shirt seam and left pant's pocket so that he could get
to the weapons he had taped to his body. There was a long gun
in his truck and C-4 in his tool box, which he would leave the
box in the truck to cover his escape.

The rain increased as he approached Emil Dakkas' home. As
Ashman got closer, he began to pay more and more attention to
the surroundings and the layout. He made two pass-bys
because all the houses in Emil's development looked the same.
There was nothing out of the ordinary there; no construction
workers, delivery men, or utility trucks.

He came in through the overgrown lawn of the house in the
back, keeping flat against the garage so that he was visible from
only the most limited angle. In his canvas tool bag was an A1-
AW sniper rifle to which he had attached a suppressor. The rifle
took a ten-round magazine, but Ashman used a five-round clip
to accommodate larger rounds with greater stopping power. He
had four loaded magazines with him.

The dark and rain were good cover, but made his view of
things difficult. Ashman unscrewed the telescopic sight from
his rifle and used it to reconnoiter Dakkas' property. The front
porch light was on. Ashman could read the date on the newspaper lying on the front porch. He waited. There was nobody
at home. Then a woman pulled up and went inside, picking up
the newspaper on her way.

Something was wrong, Ashman thought. Where's the dog? The big Dane would have been running and jumping, and Emil's wife would have let him out or he would have been barking at the door. Maybe he was at the vet? But the odds were against it.

Almost immediately after she was inside, Dakkas drove around the corner. He parked behind Sonny's car and got out. Emil's jacket was open and the headlights of his car were on delay. He was carrying two plastic bags and he had his keys in his right hand.

Ashman wasn't sure of the game, but something told him he had to get inside fast. He went through the backyard and was coming in as Dakkas opened the front door.

Emil Dakkas was calling, "Hi, honey." His eyes turned towards Ashman at the back door. He dropped his bags and cleared his Sig Sauer .45, but Sonny, whoever she was, went down prone, shooting as she did.

She had a silencer on her weapon. The first shot missed, but the second hit Dakkas in the shoulder, blowing a fist-sized hunk of flesh out his back and against the wall. Black Talon rounds, Ashman told himself as he went down behind the counter.

Isabella Enchant rolled on her right shoulder and fired at Ashman. Her shots tore a hole in the corner of the wall. He quickly withdrew to the back doorway. Dakkas was down and trying to drag himself to cover, but got off two shots left handed.

Ashman didn't know who his enemy was, but he knew she was good. Dakkas was already done or soon would be. The big dog was over to his right, bleeding out onto the kitchen floor.

There was no movement. Ashman could hear Dakkas breathing badly. Would she want both of us, he wondered, or just to finish Dakkas? Where was her back-up? Who was she? Ashman withdrew, belly-crawling backwards out of the door.

He had part of an answer to the bigger question. There was somebody big in this game since they wanted Dakkas out. The lady shooter would tell him who that was, or her back-up would.

Ashman rushed out of the yard and halfway around the house. From his new position he could see both the front and back doors. It was still raining, but the wind had changed and it was coming down at a slant.

He had a clear view to where the shooter was. Ashman saw her come up into a crouch. She was moving toward the front of the house to finish Dakkas.

He shot her with his long gun. She cried out and went down. There was blood on the wall behind her. He couldn't see Dakkas, but from the fact that he was not fighting back, Ashman knew that he was finished.

"Oh, boys," Isabella called, "is this any way to treat a lady?" She wondered who sent the one outside. Isabella dragged herself to the front door and was up hopping towards her car. Ashman wanted her alive. He shot her in the foot.

"Fuck!" Isabella said as she went down. She was squirting blood, but shot a burst at his last position.

Ashman was careful even though he knew he was in control. He had good cover and as she shot wildly through the rain,

Ashman knew that her concentration was fading. He changed his angle and shot her in the other foot. "I'm done, damn it!" she yelled, throwing her weapon down.

Isabella pushed herself up into a sitting position against the porch railing and took a tourniquet out of her kit. "I'm done. Last dance," she called.

He went up in the tree and waited for her back-up to arrive. The police would probably not come since there were only a few loud shots by Dakkas. Both he and the woman and him were using suppressors and it was raining hard.

No one came. That told him that Dakkas and the woman were both cut adrift. He remembered the C-4 explosives in his case and thought about doing them both, but then he saw her get up and try again.

She got near her car, but faded and went down alongside it. As Ashman came around from the back, he could see her put her 9mm in her mouth.

He tried to confuse her as he came around from the rear. "Who do I call? You're bleeding bad." Ashman wanted what she could tell him. "Back-up. I'm your back-up!" he tried.

She lowered her weapon. "Thank God," Isabella said as she aimed her tiny back-up with her other hand. He saw it and shot her dead. Then he drove up to the shopping center and called the police from the pay phone. If Dakkas lived, he could take the blame.

Ashman drove away from the dead woman lying in the rain, from Dakkas and from Orr, away from the Major and Maya, and away from those who had called him their friend. He drove until he was too tired to drive anymore, tired from the killing and the rain and the never-ending twists and turns, placed one upon another.

He drove off the highway and looked for a place to stop. There was a roadside bar up ahead on the right. The neon light was flashing. Ashman went down the steps and they let him in.

"Just closing," the doorman said.

"I need a beer," Ashman told him as he walked in. It was cold and dark.

"Bottle or draft?" the barkeep asked.

"As long as it's cold."

"I heard that. Eggs Doyle?" the barkeep asked.

Ashman looked at him.

"Boiled eggs," the barkeep said again pointing to the jar.

"Another beer," Ashman said. "Pour me two."

Safe

Ashman drank the first beer quickly. He was hungry, but the kitchen was closed and he could not bring himself to eat anything from the glass jar at the end of the bar.

He felt tangled-up as he drove away. He had his battles and his victories, but he still did not have his enemy. Ashman looked for a place to sleep as the road turned down and to the left. There was a hotel across the highway, but he passed it by and drove on for two more hours.

Ashman awoke and left before dawn. As he drove along, he thought how it was not the Major's world he had been in, but the General's or Fallon-Feenane's . He wondered how far back it had been their world. Had they put him in the Elms? Were they coming after him now, moving him underground? He thought about killing the General with a steel rod through his head and choking Fallon to death with Metamucil, watching him suffocate on the expanding mass of psyllium husks.

The Major, Isabella, Lorraine, Sabatino, and Frankie Cigars were gone. Orr was out of the picture. Dakkas was dead or dying. Doyle was dead. They were all wasted or soldout, but used-up for sure. He thought about the dead and the dying he had seen before, friends crying-out in their last agony, and strangers left to the rats. Didn't they all think they'd be the last one around to tell about it?

"Make sure the body bag feels right when you send it home," he said out loud. He remembered the woman he had shot at Dakkas and wondered whether she was still lying in the rain.

Ashman drove all day and then holed-up for a week in the end room of a bad motel. He was ready for a war, but nobody came.

Time went by. Maya, Venudo, and the others were getting to be background noise the longer he stayed away. "Eggs Doyle," he said to himself when he thought that. Goddamn.

He took a trip to Disney and registered under the name of Kyle Coates, but nothing happened. He was bored and restless. He found an alligator refuge from the brochures in the coffee shop and went out there.

Ashman walked along the trails and watched the feeding time. There were some babies and some big ones and one old gator all scarred up, the obvious bull of the group.

There was a notch under the overhangs and he waited there until the staff at the refuge started paying attention to him. Then he went back to his motel room and slept with the air-conditioning off. The was a good one because he could see the way in and the way out.

He knew they could still come for him at any time at any place. Maybe they were keeping him around as the one to blame or maybe they were getting around behind him. Ashman grew a mustache and colored his hair dark. He wore a pair of store-bought glasses and walked differently.

He still had bad dreams, running, dying, watching your friends who had your face, dying dreams. Sometimes he had the drowning dreams that started in the Elms. Ashman knew that was a debt that still needed repaying.

One morning he woke up knowing it was time to go away again. He never could stay in one place too long. He knew that was crazy, but that was what kept him alive. He wanted to go where it was warm and to be there fast.

There was a shuttle to Miami and he took that. There were too many things going on in Costa Rica. Maybe he'd run into some of his Cuban friends, he thought, but Alpha 66 had become "Route 66," a bad old television show. He checked into the Eden Roc under the name of Glassman and ate salami and eggs.

That night Ashman woke at 2:30 with searing face pain. He thought maybe it was his sinuses or that he had been grinding his teeth. He put a hot towel on his temples and took four Advils.

When the pain did not abate, Ashman filled his mouth with hot water to check for an abscess. The pain surged. "Fuck!" he said. "It's root canal time." He tapped his teeth with a spoon and found the right one. The pain was excruciating.

Ashman took a 2 mg. Dilaudid from his kit and called the

front desk. There was a dentist on call, but Ashman got an answering service that told him he couldn't be seen until eight o'clock the next morning.

The drug dulled the pain to a throbbing. Ashman thought about treating himself, but knew he didn't have the right tools or IRM.

When the searing pain came back, Ashman popped another orange pill and opened the phone book. There were four dentists offering twenty-four hour emergency service. He tried them all. One phone number directed him to the nearest hospital, one number was disconnected, and two had answering services that said the dentist would call him back.

The second Dilaudid made Ashman jumpy so that he walked around and around his hotel room. At seven, Dr. Carillo called him back. "There's a surcharge for an emergency visit," he told Ashman. "What's the problem?"

"I need a root canal."

"I'm not an endodontist, but I can take a look at it and give you some temporary relief. Cash, or credit card."

"Fine. I'll take a cab," Ashman told him. "I'm at the Eden Roc."

Ashman took another Dilaudid and went downstairs for a cab. It was early, but the taxis were lining up. Old women were out in white walking shoes. Tourists were going out to breakfast. He thought he saw someone he knew across the street, but it was a stranger.

The next cab pulled up. The driver was a woman wearing a leather cap. She leaned out at Ashman "Where?" she asked with a Carribean lilt.

Ashman told her and asked how long it would take to get there.

"That's about forty minutes," she answered.

He handed her two twenties. "The faster the better," he told her.

"I heard that." She said. "You mind if I smoke?"

Ashman said "no" and she lit up. He noticed she had little growths on her neck like the woman at the Elms. She put the radio on and sang with it, changing stations when the music stopped.

The dentist's office was a white stucco building with a black iron gate. Dr. Carillo answered the door wearing his white smock and Bermuda shorts. He was a white-haired man wearing lots of gold. "Come right in," he said.

"Thanks, Doc," Ashman told him.

Dr. Carillo took Ashman to the operatory and came back gloved and with goggles. "Which tooth?" he asked.

"Upper right," said Ashman pointing at it.

"We'll get right at it. I'll take a picture. You want gas?"

"I'm fine," Ashman answered.

"Judging by your pupils you are. You on anything? Any allergies? Heart problems?" Dr. Carillo asked.

"I self-medicated until I got here, but other that that. I'm fine."

The dentist put a lead apron on Ashman and stepped out of the room. While the x-ray developed, Dr. Carillo took his dental mirror and tapped three teeth. Ashman sat with his .25 surreptitiously pointing at the dentist's groin. The pain in the last tooth was excruciating.

"I guess that's it. You thought it was the tooth next to it, but that's probably referred pain," Carillo said. He held up the x-ray on the light box so Ashman could see. "Actually this one has been done before. You see the gutta percha?" He rolled the 'r' when he said it.

"Which means?"

"Which means either they didn't get all of the canal, you see the way it turns at the end, or it's gone bad, a periapical lesion. I'm going to open it up and let it drain. Put a sedative in. You should see somebody today or tomorrow." He wrote a name down on his card. "Dr. Greene, he's near your hotel. We went to school together."

Ashman heard him click in the cartridge of Novocaine. "I'll have you comfortable in a minute," the dentist said "You're not allergic to Novocaine are you?" He pulled his patient's lip while he injected him around the teeth and into the roof of his mouth.

Dr. Carillo injected the pulp, and Ashman jumped. The dentist saw his gun and fell back. "I don't keep any cash or drugs here," he said.

"You got the wrong idea," Ashman said.

"No, you got the wrong idea. You better leave. I'm calling the cops."

"My I.D. is in my jacket," Ashman told him.

"Meaning what?"

"I'm a police officer."

"And that gives you the right to..."

"Need a dentist."

"Put the gun away so I can get this over with," Dr. Carillo said. He put in a sedative packing and wrote a script for penicillin and one for Dolobid for pain. "Get these filled. Find another endodontist from the phone book, please. Dr. Greene is a friend of mine."

"How much do I owe you?"

"It's one hundred and fifty dollars. Mail it to me."

Ashman went out and looked for a cab. There was one coming up across the street, but it was occupied. He walked until he came to a shopping center near the overpass for the highway back to his hotel. The shopping center was a small one: a hobby shop, Chinese restaurant, bakery, and video store. One of the stores was vacant.

There were three cars in the front parking lot and a delivery truck and a tan Pinto in the rear. He hot-wired the Pinto and drove back, leaving it five blocks from the hotel with the engine running.

When he got back to his room, he took another Dilaudid and went down to the pharmacy in the hotel lobby. The Vietnamese pharmacist told him to take a loading dose of the anti-inflammatory, to take the Vicillin until it was finished, and to drink plenty of water. He said his brother was a dentist, but he used

Dr. Rhome.

Ashman took the penicillin and another Dilaudid and slept until five. Then he showered and walked down to the ocean.

"It's not safe," said the two old men who walked by. "It's not safe," they said to each other.

"Nowhere's not safe," Ashman answered, but they were hard of hearing.

The sun was coming down as Ashman walked by the water's edge. He felt someone walking up behind him. He could see the shadow of a large knife. Ashman stepped to the outside and brought his hand up with the .25 in it.

"Excuse me," the man behind him said. He walked by, carrying his tackle box and rod, and a large silver fish he meant to clean.

Bernsie

He stayed in Miami. It was warm and as good a place as any. Ashman knew that there was no place in this world that they couldn't find him with their Keyhole 11 satellites, or whatever else NSA had come up with. "A whole channel especially devoted to you," Major Coates once said. "There's no E and E. You can't escape or evade. There's no place you can hide," the Major had told him with a laugh.

Ashman walked around, read the paper, and drank beer. He went to the movies. He amused himself with how they'd come for him, a claymore mine on the shuffleboard court, and 'ka-blam,' lots of feet with white socks and sandals raining down. Or they could be less dramatic, he thought, a long-range shot like the ones he had made before.

Or they could reinvest him, giving him over to the Mafia as payback for Frankie Cigars, or as a sweetener in a new deal. Best job he'd ever seen was Bernsie taking a guy out as he came

off the plane in a pineapple shirt. He used a light load .22 caliber through a hot dog roll, a fucking hot dog roll.

It was time to go. He took the morning flight out. It was
crowded: tired travelers, tanned tourists, a fat man and wife
wearing matching cowboy boots. Ashman looked for the signs
that they were dangerous, had an aura about them, people who
never crossed their legs, one furtive look.

He had yogurt and some nuts and read magazines on the trip.
When the flight landed, Ashman stayed in the middle of the
group. He rented a car and went to see an old friend.

Bernstein's Hardware Store was in the middle of a second-
rate commercial block. The entrance of the store was down
some steps. No bell rang when Ashman opened the door which
made Ashman smile. If Bernsie was still Bernsie, he could tell
somebody was coming a block away.

"Hey, hey," Bernsie said when he saw Ashman. He was a
tall, gray-haired man, almost six-foot-seven. He closed the distance between the two of them in one stride to shake hands.
"How are you, boy?" Bernsie said. "How are you? They send
ya here ta kill me?" he asked, laughing.

"Not hardly, Bernsie," Ashman answered. "I'm just
cruisin'."

"Cruisin' and bruisin'. I hear they're usin' the enemy to do
their dirty work now. Ain't that some shit, using the VC?"
Bernsie went back to mixing a can of paint. "But I figured
they'd make an exception in my case. It'd hardly be right that
way, sending some yellow bastard in black pajamas to off me."

"You'd smell a slope a mile away, Bernsie."

"I'm getting old," Bernsie told him.

"You?"

Bernsie held the green paint on the stirrer stick to the paint chart. "That's the name of the game. Lying low enough to get old. Me? I'm gettin' scratchy." He paused. "I mean, itchy now and then. You wanna beer?"

He went in the back and brought out two amber bottles. "Made it myself. It's my new hobby, makin' beer. I tried wine-making, but I didn't have the patience. Cheers," he said. He handed Ashman one. They raised their bottles to each other.

"May the right people die," Bernsie said, taking a long drink. "You heard from Doc or anybody?" he asked.

"Doc's retired. Knoddles got it," Ashman said. "They blew her into chili."

"Fuck me. Fuck them. You looking to pay anybody back?" Bernsie asked

"Always," Ashman answered, smiling.

"Anything doing?" Bernsie finished off his beer and put the amber bottle on the shelf behind him.

"No more than usual."

"I heard that. You wanna get some dinner after I get this order together?" Bernsie asked. "I can brew some good brew, but I can't cook worth shit. I gotta pack an order. Then we can get Texmex around the corner."

"That's good," Ashman answered.

"Nuts and bolts, I love 'em. Calms the nerves. This place is third generation," Bernsie said. "But I guess it stops here. I thought my brother Lou's kid would come in, but the chain stores, they just put us out of business. Meanwhile, I'll stay open as long as I feel like it, cuttin' screens and shades and packin' up the orders."

He weighed a scoop of bolts. "Too much," he said, watching the scale tip. My old man could judge it on the mark." Bernsie reached in and took out four of the two-inch stainless steel bolts.

The first one hit Ashman in the right eye, the second in the forehead. He cleared his Glock as he fell, but lay motionless. The doorbell rang.

"Closed," said Bernsie strongly.

"Sorry," said the customer, who went away.

Bernsie came around from behind the counter with an ax. Ashman was blind, but he could hear the hardware odds and ends jingle in his old friend's pockets. It got louder as he got closer. It stopped as Bernsie reached him.

Ashman tilted his weapon up and spread out a field of fire. Any one would have done it. He hit Bernsie with three of them, the last one in the face. Bernsie's head was all over the store, but Ashman couldn't see it.

He lost consciousness and lay there. No customers came in and no help. Ashman lay there through the night until the pain woke him up. He tried to stand, but couldn't. His right eye was blind and he had a searing headache.

Pressure with an oven mitt stanched the bleeding from his eye. He knew he had no one to call it into. They would come to EVAC him and finish him off. A hospital is safe, he told himself, I've got no gunshot to alert anybody.

The sun was coming up as Ashman went outside. He had cleaned up, washing off the gunpowder smell with vinegar, and put on Bernsie's jacket and a Black and Decker hat. Ashman made it to the car. "Good to go," he said out loud.

The nausea and the pain were manageable, but he had double vision from one eye and none from the other. He drove slowly. A traffic accident could bring the police and a good cop could know something was wrong.

Ashman drove for twenty minutes and then saw a sign off to the right for a private out-patient facility. The hours were 7 a.m. to 10 p.m.. Only twenty minutes to wait. He drove over.

A well-dressed man got out of the tan Audi that pulled up to the clinic. He punched in the alarm code and opened the doors. After the lights were on inside, Ashman followed him in.

"Take a seat. I'm Dr. Bohm," the doctor said. "I'll be right with you." He went into his office and came out in his white jacket. The first thing that he did was to put a sterile gauze patch over Ashman's eye.

"Keep some pressure on." He gave him an intake form.

"I got double vision,"

"Not surprised," Staci will get your information when she gets here, which should be any minute, but let's get started."

Ashman assumed the demeanor of a compliant patient. "Thanks, Doc," he said.

They went into the second exam room. The doctor looked at

his forehead first. "How did this happen?" he asked.

"My job got caught in the turret lathe."

"How long ago?"

"Workin' the night shift. Am I gonna be all right? I ain't got no compo. I'm off the books."

Dr. Bohm cleansed the head wound area. "You're going to need x-rays and stitches. Are you covered by insurance?" he asked.

"I'm covered by the wife's, but I'll pay cash for this for the deductible."

"Let's look at the eye," the doctor said. He took away the pressure bandage. There still was a steady leakage. "It's still bleeding. "You should see an opthalmologist immediately. I can only triage you here for that."

"What's triage?" Ashman asked.

A bell sounded twice, announcing a visitor. "Good morning, Dr. Bohm," Staci called.

"Call over to the hospital and see if Dr. Prahanmansa can see Mr. Stowe." He turned back to Ashman. "We're part of the Cedars of Sinai system. They'll send transport for you. You really shouldn't drive."

"How far is it, Doc?"

"You should not drive." He touched the area around the forehead wound and Ashman winced.

Dr. Bohm had his patient lie down and sutured the forehead wound with nine stitches. He took bandages and gauze out of the cabinet on the right and put a proper pressure bandage in place on Ashman's eye. Staci, who was very tall, over six feet, stood behind Dr. Bohm, ready to assist.

"Headaches? Nausea?" Dr. Bohm asked.

"Both. And that double vision, Doc."

"Mr. Stowe needs a skull series," the doctor said.

"Dr. Prahanmansa's office called. They'll call us back in a half hour," the nurse answered.

"The service or the office?" Dr. Bohm asked her.

"The office," Staci answered. She took her patient down the hall.

"Quite a place you have here," Ashman told her.

"It's the Cedars'."

"Excuse me?"

"Cedars of Sinai."

"Oh," Ashman answered.

Staci took the x-rays and Dr. Bohm read them. "You've got a frontal hairline fracture."

"Is that bad?"

"There's no compression, so it's not pressing on your brain. You'll have bad headaches, nausea, double vision, and maybe some nervousness for a week or so."

"Dr. Prahanmansa can see Mr. Stowe at ten o'clock," Staci said as she came back in.

Ashman didn't want to be in any one place for too long. "Is there another hospital around?" he asked. "I don't like foreigners, dot heads, or whatever."

"There is, but it's almost an hour away," Dr. Bohm told him. "You're already here. I mean, you're in our system already."

Ashman stood up.

"You really shouldn't drive. If you do, it will have to be 'AMA,' against medical advice," the doctor told him.

"Do I have to sign something?"

"Yes and I'll note it in your chart." Dr. Bohm buzzed Staci to prepare the bill.

Ashman paid cash and drove over to the Community Hospital. He waited there an hour in the ER and then another hour and a half for Dr. William Sydney Porter, who diagnosed a punctured cornea and limbus and a lacerated lens. The laceration went part of the way into the anterior chamber.

Dr. Porter did laser surgery that afternoon on the basis of the credit card which bore the name, "Henry Ott." Ashman lay flat until the early morning, when he sneaked out of the hospital, switched cars in the parking lot, and drove away with his right eye covered.

Return

Ashman's head hurt and he was dizzy. His patched eye throbbed and his other eye ached as it tried to compensate. He had been told to lie flat and that he needed rest, but Ashman had to get away from Baltimore.

He went down into the Chesapeake Bay Tunnel, where the lines on the walls and ceiling came together in a mock illusion. New York was too far away. D.C. was too hot. Philadelphia was close and it would look like he was going home and that would be some cover.

The trip was quick and uneventful. He stopped for coffee on the way and took more pain killers, reasonably sure that he had not been followed.

Ashman wanted a place near a hospital so that his bandages didn't look out of place. The Marriott was near Wills Eye Hospital, but it was too big with too many ways in and out.

He drove to the Doubletree Hotel at Broad and Locust Streets, but there was a fire across the street and the police were directing traffic away. There were hoses across the street, flashing lights, and trucks with their ladders up. One of the cops looked like Rosie, but she didn't see him.

The Sheraton Inn at 36th and Chestnut was close to the University of Pennsylvania Hospital and the Scheie Eye Institute. Ashman decided to go there.

"Do you have a reservation?" the desk clerk asked him. The clerk wore glasses that hung on a red string like Ashman had after killing Fulliard Stevens.

"They were supposed to call over from the hospital, social service was. Can you check the name? Scott, William?" Ashman asked.

"Like the basketball player?" the desk clerk asked.

"Who?"

"Scott Williams, used to play for the Sixers."

"Who?"

" The 76'ers. The basketball team."

"No," Ashman told him. "Last name first. William Scott. They were supposed to call over from the eye hospital."

"I'm sorry, Mr. Scott. There's no reservation and we're full-up, sir." He handed Ashman a brochure. "There are three other Sheratons here in Philadelphia."

Ashman took off his sunglasses to look at the hand-outs. His wound was oozing through the bandage.

"You all right?" the clerk asked. "My wife, she's got retinitis pigmentosa. You know, like Steve Wynn. Except we don't have them casinos," he added, laughing a little bit, but with no sound coming out. "Maybe I could put you in a double. You'll have to be out by 7 A.M. Is that acceptable?"

"That's good. "I've got to lay down. They told me that at the hospital."

"Room 2012," the clerk said, giving him the key. "You should lay down. There's room service and a soda machine in the hall. There's cable. The Sixers are on, playing the Bulls."

"Thanks. Maybe I can watch myself play."

"Right, right," the desk clerk said, laughing his silent laugh again.

Ashman went to the elevators, walking slowly to memorize the layout of the lobby, the front entrance, a fire door in one corner, and a bar off to the right. Two elevators went up to his floor, which was the second from the top. There was no mezzanine.

Room 2012 was in the corner next to the fire tower. He thought about jamming the locking mechanism of the tower door, but then he would have only the elevators as a way out.

Ashman's head was pounding and he was seeing strings of lights going on and off. He had to lie down and he tried to draw the window curtains closed. They didn't go all the way and some of the street light came in through the open corner.

The room was too open and there weren't enough angles. The beds were on fixed casters so he couldn't swing them around, and they were too low to sleep under.

Ashman removed the light bulbs from the desk lamp and the bathroom and tied them together with a piece of trash can liner, Then he folded the room-service menu, which he wedged in against the tower door and hung the bulbs from it. Anybody opening the door would have to push hard and that would send the light bulbs down.

He thought about lying down in the closet or the tub, but they were too short. After taking another painkiller, he lay prone on the floor in a combat position between the double beds with the television on and the two lights out.

Ashman knew that he was fading. He closed his eyes and fell into a quick dream. He had come in from the jungle to burn out three-hundred meters of the enemy's underground haven with acetylene. Ashman and five tunnel rats were sitting above ground. They were watching the engineers chew-up the earth with Rome plows, "hog jaws," they called them. The engineers had a ton of explosives, six blowers, and hundreds of feet of hose to make an underground firestorm.

When the tunnel fire had gone out and its poison gas had dissipated, Ashman and three other rats went downstairs, staying eight yards apart so booby traps or grenades would only get one of them. The others stayed up top to lower supplies or pull one of them out.

He was younger and more agile in his dream and there wasn't a tunnel he couldn't turn around in. It started to rain and the jungle rain was landing above ground like a string of exploding rounds. It sounded like small arms fire, "pop, pop." Ashman jumped up, thinking it was the bulbs attached to the fire door.

His head and eye hurt from the quick movement, but he was

ready. He ran into the bathroom and got into the tub in case they had placed a charge against the door. Nothing happened.

After a long wait, Ashman went back and sat on the floor beyond his bed. Perhaps they had booby-trapped the door. He called for room service and went back in to the bathroom and waited in the tub for the knock on the door.

"It's open," he called when room service knocked. "I'm in the john. There's a tip on the table. Leave it in front of the television. The Bulls are playing."

There was no explosion. Room service came and left the scrambled eggs Ashman had ordered. He ate and then made a different place where he could lie down. To his surprise, he fell asleep and dreamt again. He was with Doyle and they were playing cards.

"Last dance, boys," Doyle said as he dealt the cards out. The cards were metal soldiers like the ones on Maya's shelf.

"May the right people die," answered the person next to Ashman. He couldn't see who that was, but it felt like it was the crazy man from the hospital who smelled like cooked onions. The crazy man started dealing cards too, and the cards turned into silver fishes and golden stars as he turned them up.

"Two stars," said someone who had appeared and was cleaning the red mud from under his fingernails. The mud turned to blood as it fell out.

"Two faces," said Knoddles, who had none in the dream.

The gold stars on the cards turned over and over on their arms, making clicking sounds as they did, "click, click" like mines being sprung. They made bright light as they turned and clicked, so bright that Ashman couldn't see.

He felt himself running in the slippery mud as the turning stars went on and on like a fiery wheel. He ran faster and faster, looking for a place where he could cross over the blood red mud that appeared more and more as he ran, running through tunnels underground and over it.

All the ones that he had lost, and the ones that he had killed, and the ones he kept locked away in his memory ran on with him. Eggs Doyle, Knoddles, Franca, Dakkas, General Kendall, a kid, whose body had fallen apart in his arms, families in black pajamas, the phony cops, Cambodian mayors without heads, Major Coates, and the woman assassin. And as they ran, they all turned over like the metal soldier cards being dealt out, their faces up and down, shining like the stars and the little fishes and bleeding.

"One hand left and one hand right," said Fallon-Feenane. He was dealing the soldier cards on to a table that was Ashman's trunk, which he had never opened since the war and was locked in the cellar in a stucco house in Astoria, Queens.

He ran with the hollow metal men, in and out of them like they were standing still. Fallon had monkey's paws and tiger's claws and the eyes of the Lurps who were never coming back: Metaphor, Tubman, and Smiley, who was Orr. Fallon laughed and laughed. "Cigar, boy?" he asked, firing one up and blowing out smoke that was like acetylene.

Ashman reached inside his shirt in his dream for his killing knife. He was cold, deep down cold, and his killing knife was so hot that the handle burned him when he touched it. And when he dropped that knife, it came to life and reared up and hissed at him like a cobra, but with Fallon's face. Then there were two of the hissing, man-faced cobra knives. Then ten, then thousands of them, squirming and wriggling and hissing and making formations which Ashman tried to read, but they all were turning and turning for him in a tunnel that had smooth narrow walls. The tunnel was turning, too and it went on and on and he could not escape.

A hole in the tunnel opened off to the right, and Ashman ran for it. But the sanctuary that had opened up for him had sharp snapping teeth and he had no place to run. He started to roll away and drown like at the Elms, which woke him up, soaked with the horror and the terror that had been his dreams for as long as he could remember.

Ashman quickly toweled off the sweat and took the elevator down to the parking garage. After getting a cold soda from the vending machine, he walked up the ramp without checking out. He meant to pay Mr. Fallon-Feenane a visit and hurt him bad.

The transparent tape he had placed on his vehicle was unbroken. He looked behind the wheels and at the undercarriage and unlocked the doors from ten feet away before getting in and turning the key.

"They can't even cross the street without doing it in a double inverse helix," Doc had said. "And they can't even make the sign of the cross without using both hands. Ashman went back to Washington to find out who they were.

On and On

His trip to Washington was an easy one, except for having to turn his head so his good eye could see what his bad eye couldn't. As he drove on, he felt angrier and angrier, and stronger.

No one picked him up as he approached the Pentagon or followed him in after he parked in the visitors lot. Ashman went to the main desk and asked for Major Coates. When he was asked to sign-in, he wrote "Mr. Fallon-Feenane." He walked back out and waited in his car with his .45 in his right hand and his back-up piece within reach.

A Crown Victoria pulled-up. "Quite a sense of humor," Fallon said to Ashman as he rolled down his window. "Let's have a little chat," he smiled. "And no dramatics, please." Ashman was happy to get closer.

The driver, who was big with a crewcut and square hands,

opened the back door of the blue Crown Victoria. Ashman could see the outline of his shoulder holster. Fallon turned toward him, "Glad to have you back."

"I'm retired," Ashman told him.

"Retired?" asked Fallon. "As of when?"

"As of when I killed the last man you sent for me."

"That's quite paranoid," Fallon answered, smiling again. "But that's one of your charms. General Kendall is looking forward to seeing you again." Fallon motioned to his crewcut driver. They went on in silence.

As they got within a mile of General Kendall's home, another blue Crown Victoria pulled up. It followed closely behind them and then pulled in front as they came to the macadam road that went up to the General's black iron gate. Both cars slowed on the pebbles that covered the road up to the house.

"Major Coates was only here twice," Fallon said as they stopped.

"Your weapons, please," the crewcut spoke up.

Ashman passed them over except for the razor-sharp piece of bone taped to his ribs. The two men who were in the car following him had gotten out and were on the porch. They looked like a pair of offensive linemen, both six-foot-five and with thick necks. By the way their jackets hung, Ashman could tell they carried machine pistols, either MAC 10's or Ingrams.

"Will you get this thing washed?" Fallon said to his driver as he got out. "It's filthy, particularly the windows." He motioned for Ashman to come with him.

A porch wrapped around the General's house, so Ashman couldn't see all that he wanted to. One of the linemen held the front door for them as they went in. The door had beveled glass which caught the light like a prism and the transom had colored panes. Ashman looked for the alarm system, but couldn't see any.

A woman in her fifties came down the stairs. Mrs. Kendall had on riding clothes, and her reddish hair was in a bun. "Good morning," she said. "You can put your coats in the hall closet." She left to answer the phone.

Ashman went to hang up his jacket. The hall had oriental runners on the floor with thick padding underneath. The closet smelled like cigars and potpourri. He would have liked to gather more intelligence, but Fallon had started down the hall to the sunlit room where General Kendall sat in his shirt sleeves.

"Sit down, Captain Ashman," General Kendall said. He closed the curtains so Ashman couldn't see the big man with the thick neck, who waited outside on the flagstone patio.

"My 'AAR', General Kendall?" Ashman asked. He used the military term as much to exclude Fallon as to acknowledge the General's use of his old rank.

"No 'After Action Report' is necessary. We're here to talk about the future. Although it does somehow run together, doesn't it?"

Fallon sat down next to General Kendall. "I work for General Kendall. There may be things for you to do from time to time. You'll be speaking to me after today."

Ashman couldn't tell who was speaking for whom. "Like

Major Coates?" he asked.

"The Major's retired," Fallon said.

"I wanted to see your face, Captain, and for you to see me," General Kendall said. "Let's go for a little walk."

Ashman followed the General out onto the patio, thinking about cutting Fallon's throat with the bread knife on the kitchen counter or the bone knife strapped to his ribs. They went through a half-open dutch door which was painted gray like the woodwork in the hall. Fallon stayed behind.

"That's my favorite room, that little nook," the General said. He gestured with his cigar, "I see that you've been in the mud and blood." Ashman nodded.

As the two of them walked along the flagstone patio, a big striped cat came down across the wall and jumped up onto the bottom half of the gray dutch door. "He's a ratter," Kendall observed. "But there's no work for him now. Helena boards her horses now. There's no feed, so no more rats," He paused, tapping off his cigar's ash. "You don't like my breakfast guest?"

"I don't like people trying to kill me."

"Baltimore? Mr. Fallon told me about that. Your friend Bernsie just lost it there."

"Or anybody else, General Kendall. Your lady's dead, too, and probably Dakkas and Orr."

"It's a pity. Isabella was quite good. It's her position you're here for. She cleaned things up for me, like Major Coates and his mess. The others became part of that mess, all of them,

Dakkas, Orr, Lorraine Knoddles, your friend Doyle. It's what got you in that hospital. Major Coates' little circle jerk turned into a blood orgy. He was a 'self-aggrandizing careerist,' I'm afraid." General Kendall waited for a comment from Ashman about his quotation. "William Stevenson said that," the General explained, "in his writing about Intrepid."

"I'm more Wild Bill Hickcock than Wild Bill Donovan," Ashman answered, confusing Donovan for William Stephenson, who was Intrepid. "I killed your cleaning lady and now you want me to be the new one?"

"In a manner of speaking. I have lots of the all-American type like the one who drove you and Mr. Fallon here this morning."

"And the one on the patio?" Ashman asked.

"Actually there's two on the patio," the General said smiling, "And one at the tree line." he added. "We need a tomcat, somebody waiting for the rats to come out of their holes. These are complicated times. It goes on and on. While we wonder whether our democracy will consent to its survival, Flight 800 turns into the President getting a blow-job turns into Iraq. Things get messy along the way, or somebody loses it like Major Coates. That puts you at my right hand, and from time to time back in the mud and blood. And perhaps I might provide you with some protection to keep the splatter off," he added, smiling again.

A reddish chipmunk came across the flagstone and went into its underground burrow as they went inside. Fallon walked Ashman back up the hall.

One of the linemen was waiting for them. He tossed Ashman the car keys. The fact that they had brought his car up, said they were going to get rid of him immediately if he said no.

Fallon came down off the porch with the square-handed driver a few steps behind. "Like the General said, we'll be fine. You can call me Feenane."

Ashman drove off, following the stone driveway and then the macadam road out to the Beltway and I-95 north. He thought about his meeting with Fallon and the General. Who was the cat and who was the rat?

He had seen all of it over and over again. Loyalty and betrayal bleeding one into another. Ashman thought about walking away from General Kendall, Fallon, all of them. But he knew that he couldn't do that without coming apart. He needed the conflict and the killing and he hated them, all of the Generals and all of the Fallons, for knowing it and making it so.

* * *

Ashman stayed on the road for three days before going back to Maya's. He drove through her neighborhood twice when he arrived and parked around the corner.

There was a different van in the driveway next door, but there was a car seat in the back and a school bag. The van had dealer's plates. It was probably a loaner. There was another car across the street. Ashman thought about checking that, too, but the man who lived across the street with the lame dog, got in it and drove away.

He felt centered being back at Maya's and knowing that General Kendall would have him in the field again. He thought about the metal soldiers on the window sill and how Maya had put up with his craziness.

She had the downstairs lights on. Ashman went around back and checked the shed and the back door. Everything was secure. It felt good to be back. He went in.

Maya had armed the alarm and the shower upstairs was running. Ashman opened the frig and took out a piece of cold chicken, which he ate in the next room, looking at the mail. He drank a glass of ice water and went upstairs.

As he came down the upstairs hall, he heard the shower and then, as he came to the bedroom, he saw the dark hair of a man sleeping face down in his bed. Ashman thought of Franca as he pulled back the hammer on his .45 and stood in the doorway.

The shower stopped. Ashman waited for Maya to come out with a towel wrapped around her head, her skin flushed from the hot water. Sometimes she wore his slippers. When she came out, he would kill the dark-haired man sleeping on his side of the bed.

The bathroom door opened. It was Al Couington. Ashman didn't recognize him, and aimed the big automatic at his heart.

"Hey, hey man," Couington yelled, "What the fuck you doin? I'm here with Venudo."

"Yo," Venudo said, sitting up in the bed.

"Cowboy over here was going to blow me away," Al told him.

"Both of you," Ashman answered.

"That's fucking nuts. We're babysittin'," Venudo told him.

"Your lady's in the middle room. She called me this afternoon, nervous She said some government-looking types have been following her since last night. As big as football players, she said. I thought you'd want us to baby-sit her."

"You did the right thing," Ashman replied. He turned to leave.

"Where you goin'?" Venudo asked.

"Me? I'm going to go sit in the waves and drink some gin."

Ashman stopped by the shelf downstairs and put one of the metal soldiers in his pocket. "And after I've had my fill of gin, I'm going to kill somebody," he said. "In fact, I'm going to kill them all."

Don't miss the first in the
Lucas Rook Series

Richard Sand's
PRIVATE JUSTICE

Available this Spring

Turn the page for a taste of it

Someone is killing the little girls

Chapter One

There was a picture on the front page of The New York Post Kirk and Lucas Rook receiving their gold shields. The idea was from the higher-ups. "Good 'P.R.',", someone downtown said.

They had gone through the academy together and walked the same beat. For a while they even rode the same blue and white before Kirk got transferred downtown and Luke sent up to Washington Heights. The dated sisters and Kirk married the smiling one whose name was Ann.

On the day that Kirk Rook was shot to death outside The Sephora Club, his twin came rushing down, the lights on his unmarked flashing, his siren screaming, him knowing that death was coming and fearing it more than his own.

"I won't be there to see him go," said Lucas Rook over and over as he came screeching to see himself laying in the spread-

ing pool of blood.

But Mercy gave them a final gift, and for one last time they both still breathed. Lucas held his brother to him. No word was said until he let him go.

"An ugly business," spoke the ranking officer on the scene.

"Anybody would have taken him for me," was all that Lucas said.

Rook turned in his badge after his twin, his finer half he thought, was laid to rest by white-gloved hands. In the crucible of that moment, Lucas began his cruel pursuit.

Each one died who had caused the death. Some in daylight, some in stealth. The last one dragged in front of The Sephora Club.

The tie between the two of them who had played cowboy games and dated sisters and received their gold shields on the same day and who had walked the beat and rode the same blue and white, became a mysterious one. One twin a phantom up ahead or a pale shadow in an empty room. And Lucas Rook now at the hire of strangers, and with a need for revenge that had not left.

* * *

Lucas Rook wanted to look at the scene before he met with his potential client. He wanted to get the feel of where the little girl was dropped like a bag of rocks. He traveled Route 6 both east and west before he stopped and walked back to the flowered cross. It was next to the sign for Herring River Road where the two-lane road became a bridge over abandoned railroad tracks.

Almost a year had passed since Heather Raimondo was found in a burlap bag by the side of the road. Friends and relatives still came to keep the blooms alive on the makeshift monument. Rook knew better, that soon enough the fresh flowers would be replaced by plastic ones and then by none at all.

The abduction and murder of Heather Raimondo would exist only in the tortured minds of the little girl's parents and the killer's remembrance. The police file would be closed. Perhaps the family would keep her room the way it was. Rook wondered if the murderer kept a scrapbook or some other souvenir, a lock of hair perhaps.

He walked along the shoulder of the road and back into the overgrown brush and bushes, pushing aside some brambles and low-growing poison ivy with his cane. The sun was beginning to go down and the mosquitoes coming up as he made his way across the two-lane highway. The view from that side of the road was the same, but up about a hundred yards he found a small path into the weeds. There was a semi-circle of bricks and a half dozen beer cans, light beer, and an empty pack of Marlboro Lights. College boys or dead-end kids with dead-end jobs. It didn't matter which.

Rook wondered why the killer hadn't thrown his bag of death over the bridge. There was high grass on the railroad underneath. A low fog hung like cigarette smoke. Perhaps he didn't have the time, or perhaps in his insane mind he didn't want to hurt the little girl.

Lucas Rook saw a bat swoop down to feed when he crossed back over to get his car. As he drove away, the sky had turned to asphalt and there was no moon.

Check out these other fine titles by
Durban House at your local book store.

Exceptional Books
by
Exceptional Writers

MR. IRRELEVANT by Jerry Marshall.

Sports writer Paul Tenkiller and pro-football player Chesty Hake have been roommates for eight career seasons. Paul's Choctaw background of poverty and his gambling on sports, and Hake's dark memories of his mother being killed are the forces which will make their friendship go horribly wrong.

Chesty Hake, the last man chosen in the draft, has been dubbed Mr. Irrelevant. By every yardstick, he should not be playing pro football. But, because of his heart and high threshold for pain, he preservers.

Paul Tenkiller has been on a gravy train because of Hake's generosity. Gleaning information vital to gambling on football, his relationship with Hake is at once loyal and deceitful.

Then during his eighth and final season, Hake slides into paranoia and Tenkiller is caught up in the dilemma. But Paul is behind the curve, and events spiral out of his control, until the bloody end comes in murder and betrayal.

OPAL EYE DEVIL by John Lewis.

From the teeming wharves of Shanghai to the stately offices of New York and London, schemes are hammered out to bankrupt opponents, wreck inventory, and dynamite oil wells. It is the age of the Robber Baron — a time when powerful men lie, steal, cheat, and even kill in their quest for power.

Sweeping us back to the turn of the twentieth century, John Lewis weaves an extraordinary tale about the brave men and women who risk everything as the discovery of oil rocks the world.

Follow Eric Gradek's rise from Northern Star's dark cargo hold to the pinnacle of high stakes gambling for unrivaled riches.

Aided by his beautiful wife, Katheryn, and the devoted Tong-Po, Eric fights for his dream and for revenge against the man who left him for dead aboard Northern Star.

ROADHOUSE BLUES by Baron Birtcher.

From the sun-drenched sand of Santa Catalina Island to the smoky night clubs and back alleys of West Hollywood, Roadhouse Blues is a taut noir thriller that evokes images both surreal and disturbing.

Newly retired Homicide detective Mike Travis is torn from comfort of his chartered yacht business and into the dark, bizarre underbelly of LA's music scene by a grisly string of murders.

A handsome, drug-addled psychopath has reemerged from an ancient Dionysean cult leaving a bloody trail of seemingly unrelated victims in his wake. Despite departmental rivalries that threaten to tear the investigation apart, Travis and his former partner reunite in an all-out effort to prevent more innocent blood from spilling into the unforgiving streets of the City of Angels.

Coming January, 2001 from
Durban House Publishing Company

DEATH OF A HEALER by Paul Henry Young

Paul Henry Young's compelling tale Death of a Healer clearly places him into the spotlight as one of America's premier writers of medical thrillers. The Story stunningly illuminates the darker side of the medical world in a way nonfiction could never accomplish.

Death of a Healer chronicles the lifelong journey of Jake Gibson, M.D., diehard romanticist and surgeon extraordinaire, as he struggles to preserve his professional oath against the avarice and abuse of power so prevalent in present-day America.

Follow Jake as he runs headfirst into a group of sinister medical and legal practitioners determined to destroy his beloved profession. Events begin spinning out of control when Jake uncovers a nationwide plot by hospital executives to eliminate certain patient groups in order to improve the bottom line.

With the lives of his family on the line, Jake invokes a self-imposed banishment as a missionary doctor and rediscovers his lifelong obsession to be a trusted physician.

Death of a Healer is a masterfully constructed suspense novel; packed with the kind of gritty authenticity only a gifted writer can portray.